RETURN TO SPINNER'S INLET

Return to Spinner's Inlet

STORIES

DON HUNTER

TOUCHWOOD

Edited by Marlyn Horsdal
Designed by Colin Parks
Proofread by Claire Philipson

LIBRARY AND ARCHIVES CANADA CATALOGUING IN PUBLICATION
Title: Return to Spinner's Inlet : stories / Don Hunter.
Names: Hunter, Don, 1937- author.
Identifiers: Canadiana 20190103604 | ISBN 9781771513081 (softcover)
Classification: LCC PS8565.U5785 R48 2019 | DDC C813/.54—dc23

TouchWood Editions gratefully acknowledges that the land on which we live and work is within the traditional territories of the Lkwungen (Esquimalt and Songhees), Malahat, Pacheedaht, Scia'new, T'Sou-ke, and W̱SÁNEĆ (Pauquachin, Tsartlip, Tsawout, Tseycum) peoples.

We acknowledge the financial support of the Government of Canada through the Canada Book Fund and the Canada Council for the Arts, and of the Province of British Columbia through the British Columbia Arts Council and the Book Publishing Tax Credit.

  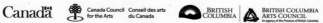

PRINTED IN CANADA

23 22 21 20 19   1 2 3 4 5

For June, always,
and for Susie and Taryn

Contents

Swede Down

It was commonly agreed in Spinner's Inlet that Rachel Spinner should be the main speaker at Svensen's funeral.

The Swede, who had sat down on a driftwood log on the beach in Spinner's Inlet, placed his twenty-four-inch-bar Husqvarna chainsaw carefully by his boots and not risen again, had been sent on his way not exactly with the Viking funeral that he had suggested—being cremated along with his boat out on the strait so that his soul would rise with the smoke and ashes into Valhalla. That particular venue, it was pointed out to him by his elementary school-principal neighbour, Julie Clements, who had studied Norse folk history as part of her Simon Fraser

University master's program, was specifically reserved for Vikings who had died in combat. Svensen's argument that his involvement, and mostly victories, in various confrontations in logging camps from the Queen Charlottes, now Haida Gwaii, to Boston Bar and Hope made him as much a combatant as any Viking, was dismissed.

He received a ceremony at the Church in the Vale, accompanied by ABBA playing in the background, because the Reverend Amber Rawlings, overseeing the ceremony, swore that Svensen nightly played a DVD of the group from his homeland. She had chanced to see and hear it more than once through the narrow gap in the centre opening of his drapes, and she also happened to have their whole collection. As a woman of the cloth, and the daughter of the retired-but-still-resident Randall Rawlings, she held considerable clout, so "Dancing Queen" and "I Have a Dream" it was.

Rachel delivered what passed as a eulogy for Svensen before a standing-room-only audience of much of the Inlet's population and a few retired loggers, who had drifted in from here and there in the bush to see an old and respected colleague move on. Rachel spoke not with notes, but from the heart. Some found her words at times inelegant, but none could fault her accuracy. She noted that *The Tidal Times* had reported that the Swede had been taken unexpectedly.

"He made his own potato vodka, drank like a drain, and was 103. The only thing unexpected was that he was able to stand up and ambulate without help for as long as he did."

She was estimating his age—nobody really knew it, and those who had asked him did it only the once. No one objected when Rachel proposed that Svensen be buried with the Santa hat and suit that had for decades been his uniform at the community Christmas gatherings, and wearing under the suit his ripened caulk boots, logger's pants with suspender buttons, and his perpetually present red suspenders. She dwelt at some length on the running argument that Svensen had had with the late Chief Jimmy Plummer concerning the earliest arrivals on the British Columbia coast.

Svensen's case had been seriously compromised when he invoked Thor Heyerdahl's Kon-Tiki expedition as proof of Viking arrivals, conceding that while Heyerdahl was Norwegian, that was as close as you could get to being the real thing. Chief Jimmy pointed out that, according to Google—and known to anyone not as dumb as a stump—Heyerdahl's expedition occurred in 1947, when things here were already quite well settled, and that anyway, his balsa-wood raft had ended up in Polynesia. He had concluded, "And, have you never wondered why it is that we are called First Nations?"

So now their debate was over.

Several of those present volunteered to be pallbearers. Two of these were spry widows of Rachel's vintage (advanced nineties) who stepped from the ferry dressed in faded but perfectly pressed Second World War air force-blue uniforms of skirt, tunic, and cap. Each wore the two thin stripes of a second officer in the British Air Transport Auxiliary and a pilot's wings. Along with Rachel, they had been ferry pilots in that conflict, delivering, in all kinds of British weather, every make of aircraft from Spitfires to heavy bombers to airfields across the UK. Each of them had, on previous visits, shown an interest in the Swede, which had not been reciprocated. The ageing flyers would have been in the Inlet anyway, for their monthly visit, during which the three of them would remonstrate with the TV over some improbable plot point while binge-watching Rachel's carefully recorded episodes of *Coronation Street* and sipping Harveys Bristol Cream sherry.

Funeral Usher-in-Chief Samson Spinner, Rachel's nephew and now de facto elder statesman of the Spinner clan, with alarming visions of the two old lady pilots over-exerting themselves, adding to the list of dearly departed and gaining new wings, of the heavenly variety, persuaded them to park themselves in a pew by the church door.

Julie Clements, who was related to the Spinners through her father, Paul Martin, whose grandfather Henry had married Victoria Spinner in 1903—as shown in Rachel's substantial and verified genealogical collection—advised that traditionally there were six pallbearers.

The Reverend Amber Rawlings said that while she was against gambling in principle, perhaps a lottery could be held among all those wishing to tote the casket from the church out to the Wilson family pickup, an old blue-and-rust Ford thing. Rachel had dictated it would be the hearse, in the interest of economy, though the bill later presented by Charlie Wilson suggested that he, like his father, Lennie, before him, was imbued with all the

4

generosity one might expect of a Scottish banker after a poor quarter, and he and Samson would have words before reaching a settlement.

Samson muttered, "Christ!" appointed himself lead bearer and stuck the rest of the names into his golf cap for a draw.

Annabelle Bell-Atkinson, the much younger sister of a former and now late Miss Bell-Atkinson, who for decades had monitored and corrected the habits and practices of the Inlet population, hinted that the draw was fixed when her name was not pulled. When no one rose to that point, she claimed also that there was a glaring lack of diversity and inclusivity because no Muslims had been selected. When advised politely by Ali Hanif, the head of and spokesperson for the five-member Afghan refugee family who had been sponsored by a combined Lions and Legion group, that none of his Muslims had put their name forward because they felt it would be a bit presumptuous after only six months in the community, she sniffed that that was all very well, but if the family was going to integrate, as was expected of them, then it was time to get on board.

This brought a murmur from an unidentified source in the gathering that she might be a racist, which produced a contradiction from one of her twin nephews, the geeks Henry and/or Harvey—the two impossible to tell apart—who proposed that it was a momentary clash of cultures that time and generous spirits would heal. They cited statements from the prime minister about diversity as proof.

Samson muttered, "Christ!" again, and took charge. Rachel would walk ahead of the coffin followed by an honour guard of the Inlet's RCMP, Constable Ravina Sidhu in full red serge and her buddy from Depot, Constable Sammy Quan, who had negotiated a day off from the Salt Spring detachment and grabbed a water taxi.

Samson read out the names that he had picked from his cap, before stuffing them into his pocket. He led the way on the front left handle. To his right was a close-to-retirement Dr. Timothy, recently returned from his annual sojourn to the Turks and Caicos Islands, whose frequent advice to Svensen about his drinking had been unfailingly ignored. "You can't say I didn't warn him," he whispered to Samson.

On the middle two handles were, on the left, Evelyn Spinner, daughter of the late Chief Jimmy Plummer and wife of Jackson Spinner for these past thirty years. "Dad would have wanted one of us to be a witness," she said. "They were old friends, sort of, after all." Across from her strode the Inlet's vet, Scotty McConville, with Svensen's German Shepherd, Conrad (the fourth of Svensen's shepherds so named), on a leash and looking baffled.

On the left rear was Willie Whittle, who had taken on the job at the BC Ferries booth when his father, Sebastian, had retired. (There was a letter in *The Tidal Times* wondering about a lurking nepotism at work, but a BC Ferries official assured all that the competition had been fair and square. The accusatory letter, over a name not recognized in the Inlet—nor anywhere else—had actually been placed by the paper's new owner, Silas Cotswold, who had feared the consequences of stating his apparently unfounded suspicions in a regular editorial.) At the coffin's right rear, completing the cortege, were Julie Clements's twelve-year-old twins Alun and Jillian, whom Samson, knowing their penchant for conflict over seniority—Alun was born just before midnight on New Year's Eve, Jillian one minute after—had allowed each to have a finger on the handle.

Jillian asked Samson if Svensen had signed an organ donor card and if so, which of his bits would be harvested for reuse.

"Harvested? Harvested?" Samson sputtered. Anything else he might have said was muffled by the sudden roaring overhead of a low-flying DHC-2 Beaver float plane that dipped, then soared and seemed to disappear in a silence as it passed beyond Spinner's Mountain, itself quite low. Breaths were bated while images of Mark Clements, husband of school principal Julie, wrestling with the controls of the one plane in his new charter business filled imaginations. But in less than a minute, the four-seater curled around the headland and splashed safely down in the bay.

Constable Sammy Quan took out a bugle from under his tunic and broke into a moving version of "The Last Post" in B-flat, and kept proudly repeating the final notes until Constable Ravina stepped on his foot and said, "That's good, Sammy."

As the cortege resumed, Alun asked Samson who was correct, Svensen or the late Chief Jimmy, on the matter of first arrivals.

"Later!" Samson snapped.

And later, after a communal repast of traditional Swedish dishes that Rachel had taken from a book of Swedish recipes found among Svensen's sparse belongings (only the fish balls proved a bit slippery and difficult), Samson said that all he knew about arrivals was contained in Rachel's history of the Spinner family. In 1855, twenty-six-year-old Samson had abandoned the bleak life of a collier in the mines of England's north-west county of Cumberland (now Cumbria), where the narrow seams ran for miles out under the Solway Firth and men worked the coal face with picks and shovels, on their knees, and often lying on their sides, in fetid water, for wages that barely kept a family fed. He and his nineteen-year-old bride, the former Maud Skillings, had made the arduous journey to what later would become British Columbia, and were among the first non-Indigenous settlers of the Gulf Islands. (Chief Jimmy Plummer would frequently, and patiently, remind the family of the hyphenated qualifier.)

A small rowboat had been lowered from the merchant ship they had boarded in Victoria, and the young couple had climbed down into it. Their belongings, in two trunks, had been lowered after them. The following day, after a night camped on the twenty acres they had purchased from the Hudson's Bay Company for one pound an acre—money scrimped by two generations of two families of coal miners—they had rowed out again to claim the first of their livestock: one milk cow in calf, two oxen, a crate of chickens, and a yearling bay stallion. Everything except the chickens had been shoved, protesting, off the back of the boat, and encouraged to swim.

Samson recited from memory the words in Rachel's family history. "Regrettably, both of the oxen and the stallion at first chose the opposite shore as their destination. Only after considerable and repeated efforts were we able to persuade the beasts that their health and future well-being—to say nothing of our own—would be best served by them adjusting their bearings and making their way to the flat beaches of what soon we would name, Spinner's Inlet."

Young Alun laughed. "Good thing the first Samson turned them around. Who knows where we might be living today!"

As the gathering broke up, Dr. Timothy asked, "Where's Conrad?"

The Clements youngsters found him sitting by the freshly filled grave. Conrad IV seemed to be checking the sky, where fleecy clouds were being ushered along by a soft breeze.

"What's he doing?" Alun asked.

"Duh. Looking for the angels, of course," Jillian replied.

Ali's Friend

Jack Steele was ready when Ali Hanif arrived.

Jack was a New Zealander and an exchange teacher at Spinner's Inlet Secondary School. He had assumed that, being in a sister country of the Commonwealth, he would find cricket to be a popular sport. Not so much, as he discovered. But he was not about to be deterred and had enlisted Ali to help explain the finer points.

Ali had not been Jack's first choice. Earlier, he had asked Constable Ravina Sidhu to drop by and "offer some tips to a group." Ravina turned up, thinking it likely had to do with drugs.

Instead, "Cricket?" she said. "What the hell do I . . ."

"Surely a national game," Steele said. "I mean, where are you from—Mumbai? Delhi?"

"Abbotsford," Ravina replied. "And my national game is hockey. The ice kind. UBC T-Birds for two season, and I was in line for the national team before I decided to be a cop. Cricket is daft. Five hours or more, run around shouting 'Howzat?' stop for tea . . . I think my dad still follows it. Maybe you could call him, though you'd have to pay his ferry fare. And you might have trouble understanding him—he's from Bradford."

So, no Ravina.

When he arrived, Ali had said he would willingly help but would not have much time this first day. He kept checking his watch as he explained to the assembled and mostly indifferent Grade 9 students that those things were called wickets, not sticks as one voice suggested, that the ball was not thrown at them but bowled, and he was getting on about overs and boundaries and hitting for six, when the many-times-refurbished *Gulf Queen* announced her arrival in the Inlet.

Ali left and trotted down the hill to the dock, where the passengers were streaming ashore and the soldier was turning heads. His faded camouflage top carried the marks of service abroad. He seemed distressed, staring around him, grabbing at something, at nothing, opening then closing his fists. His eyes seemed unfocused—until he saw Ali. He pushed through people to reach the Afghan, whom he folded in an embrace as tight as embraces can get.

"All right, Harry. It's all right now. You're safe," Ali said.

The soldier said, "Thank you, my friend." His face was wet.

"No, it is I who should be saying that!"

A young man standing nearby studied the scene. He carried a reporter's notebook. His boss, Silas Cotswold, owner and editor of *The Tidal Times*, had said, "People, Cameron, that's where you find the stories. Everybody has a story. Let them tell it."

Cameron Girard decided to heed that advice. As the one intern taken on by the *Times,* he needed to impress, which meant more than quoting Annabelle Bell-Atkinson after she had hunted him down to deliver "some more significant community news," mostly with herself up front.

He had already done a decent job on a welcoming piece about the Hanif family of five—Ali, his wife, Aila, two young girls, Nadia and Balour, and one younger boy, Fabian— although he sensed that there was much unsaid about their story.

Ali Hanif had been pleased with the story that Cameron had produced: straightforward, quotes exactly as he had spoken, and a suggestion that there was more to the tale than the reporter was able to tell. Now the reporter could have the rest. Ali beckoned the clearly curious Cameron over.

Cameron asked how the cricket coaching was going. Ali rolled his eyes. Then he tapped the soldier on the chest and said, "Here is your story, Cameron, and it's time that someone told it."

The story appeared in the next day's edition of *The Tidal Times,* as told by Ali.

"I lived in Kabul. I have a degree in engineering from the university there, and I was working what I thought was secretly as an interpreter for the Canadian forces. Harry was my main contact. He was Corporal Dyson. The Taliban learned of my work, and I and my family became targets. Harry became my protector. He was close by one day when an old pickup truck stopped outside my house. A young girl stepped out, and the truck left, quickly. The girl walked toward the house. She looked odd, staring straight ahead, a fixed smile, but her eyes were blank. I suspected that she was drugged. And I knew what she was wearing under her bulky, quilted jacket: a suicide-bomb pack.

"She started to open her jacket, just as Harry walked out from behind the house, carrying his assault rifle. She stared at him and put her hand on a red square on the bomb pack. Harry spoke to her, using the Pashto language I'd been helping him learn. He told her quietly that what she was about to do was against the true spirit of Islam and not what Allah wanted. I don't know if he actually believed it, but he got her attention—for a moment. While he spoke, he raised his rifle.

"He spoke to the girl again, asking her to take off the bomb pack. She smiled at him, nodded—and stabbed a finger at the red square. Harry was responding to his training. He shot her. He followed the ambulance to the hospital and waited by her bed for two days, before she died.

"She was seven years old. Her name was Aila, same as my wife. And the same age as Harry's daughter.

The bomb squad found that her device was improperly wired and would not have detonated. Harry cried. He's been crying, in a way, ever since.

"The army did try to help him, declared him as suffering from PTSD and referred him to their best doctors. But the damage was too deep. His life fell apart. He lost his wife, who left with their daughter, and his home. He had been due for promotion to sergeant. Harry said he had no interest in promotion, or anything further to do with the army. He would leave the regiment, but he insisted that the army keep their promise, that they would help interpreters and their families get to Canada, when the Canadians left. We had heard that the British were backing down on the same promise, leaving people like us to the Taliban. The army kept their promise and here we are.

"I found where Harry was living—on the streets in Vancouver—and now he has a new home, with us, for as long as he needs it."

Silas Cotswold had smiled as he read Girard's last line. "You're getting the hang of it, Cameron,"

Ali did not show at the school for the next week, and longer. With the interest in cricket receding like an outgoing tide, Jack Steele put away the bails and wickets and asked how many would be interested in starting a rugby sevens program.

Elections

Annabelle Bell-Atkinson started a bit of a flurry when she claimed in a letter to *The Tidal Times* that the absence of an elected governing body in Spinner's Inlet was a vacuum to be filled, "and as everyone is aware, nature abhors a vacuum."

The letter received a number of responses, including one from Finbar O'Toole that stated, "There is no such thing as a vacuum in nature because if there were such a thing, all the stuff around it would fall in and fill it."

However, Finbar conceded that there was merit in Miss B-A's argument, given that Spinner's Inlet is a "disorganized geopolitical unit," with most of the powers over its existence vested in the Islands Trust, a group that did not include "anyone from here, or anyone that anyone from here voted for." He immediately emailed a second, apologetic message to the *Times*, saying that he had meant "unorganized," but Silas Cotswold, sensing the potential for hostile letter responses to the first one, ditched it. Silas then wrote an editorial calling for an election to be held for the positions of mayor and four councillors, and named a date four weeks ahead. When it was pointed out to him that he was neither an elected nor appointed official and therefore lacked the authority to determine anything on anyone's behalf, he referred the critics to Annabelle Bell-Atkinson's and Finbar's original letters and said, "Somebody had to take charge, so there you go. If people in this community feel that we need a mayor, that's what we will have."

Campaigning began immediately in emails to the *Times*, some of it leaning on the need for diversity on the new council, like Gilbert Chen who owned Gilbert's Groceries. He pointed out that he is third-generation Chinese Canadian, one of whose forebears was made to pay the fifty-dollar head tax more than a hundred years ago to get into the country. Finbar O'Toole responded that while he sympathized with Gilbert's forebears, the Chinese Canadians had, rightfully, received apologies in both federal and provincial legislatures. However, he could not recall the same being extended by any premier or president to any of his native homelanders for the notices that used to appear in establishments in eastern Canada and in the United States stating "Help wanted. No Irish need apply."

The two then repaired to the Cedars pub where, after a couple of beers, Gilbert volunteered to start a petition on behalf of any Celts who still felt overlooked. Then he went to the bar, brought back two pints of perfectly poured Guinness and a brace of Jameson shooters, and declared, "*Sláinte!*" When they left the Cedars, arms linked, Gilbert suggested that Finbar set a precedent by showing up on time the next day, one of the two days a week that O'Toole drove Gilbert's delivery van.

Samson Spinner declared for mayor, as did Annabelle Bell-Atkinson. Samson's emails and posters billed him as a "luminary of the non-Indigenous First Families of the Inlet" and "inheritor and guardian of their traditions." Annabelle Bell-Atkinson questioned just how much light Samson shed on anything. She said that she was currently exploring through a DNA sample sent to Ancestry.com the possibility of an Indigenous connection in her family that, if it came back positive, would make her "part of this precious land" and thus qualified to be an overseer. She added that any traditions that needed protecting should amount to more than Samson's organizing and serving behind the cash bar at the annual Fall Festival and supervising the repainting of the Legion Hall.

The race for mayor thickened when Evelyn Spinner, née Plummer, joined in. She explained that someone who was First Nations could just as easily qualify for First Mayor. Silas Cotswold drew a load of mockery and the word "chewvanist" was spray-painted on his front window when he asked in print if Evelyn perhaps meant First Mayor-ESS. No one could be certain of the tagger's identity, but the quality of the spelling attached suspicion to O'Toole and his frequent boasts of having achieved all that he had in life despite having not gone beyond Grade 6.

But Evelyn's candidacy was short-lived. She withdrew when her husband, Jackson, showed her an impressive list of guests who had already booked and paid in advance for accommodation at their new B & B—first named J & E's and shortly thereafter renamed E & J's. They had built the B & B adjacent to their marina and were due to have a "grand opening, complete with celebrities" in a few weeks. Jackson asked her who she thought might do the beds and breakfasts and such, because *somebody* had to look after the boats and people who wanted to rent them. And had she got the celebrities lined up yet? Evelyn said the Vancouver mayor had said he would be at his holiday cabin that day and might come by.

Others declared for the top seat. The aforementioned Finbar O'Toole, whose claim that he was the Inlet's "Master of All Trades Handyperson" was rarely supported by any evidence of completed—or even started—projects, said he could, with a complex reorganization of his calendar, manage sufficient time to handle the duties of mayor, and he wondered how much the job would pay, and whether it would be a union position with pension and other benefits.

Sheila Martin, retired secondary school English teacher, whose daughter Julie Clements was the elementary school principal, posted her entry with a reminder that she knew just about everything about everyone in the community who had gone through the secondary school and her English classes in the past thirty years. In a pre-election interview, Cotswold queried if that was meant as some kind of threat. Sheila smiled.

After getting permission from their aunt Annabelle, who figured it might be an option for keeping things in the family, the Bell-Atkinson geeks jumped in for mayor, saying it was time that Spinner's Inlet stopped being a backwater of technology. That a mayor should be someone conversant with information technology and artificial intelligence, fluent in advanced communications, who knew the difference between kilobytes and kilograms, and would be able to combat any cyber-meddling by who knows whom, aimed at influencing the election results. Silas applauded the presence of such qualified candidates, until a candidacy form was ruled to be a duplicate, but no one, including the geeks, was certain whose it was, so they were both ruled ineligible.

One entrant just beat the deadline set by Cotswold. Randolph Champion declared that he represented the under-represented, the repressed, the common man (and woman), and worldwide economic inequality. He claimed that he had been one of the organizers of Occupy Wall Street in 2011, the World Trade Organization riots in Seattle before that (he had protest signs and placards in his garage that could be real, or not), and because of his background had regularly been refused employment by "the usual suspects in the ranks of capitalism," who, by rejecting him were both "perpetrating and prolonging pre-existing prejudices." No one could recall any employment that Randolph had applied for in the three years he and his wife and three offspring had lived in the Inlet.

"Let democracy show us the way," his poster ended.

"Or the door," an anonymous hand added.

Charlie Wilson started running a book, offering odds ranging from even money on Samson and Sheila to fifty-to-one on Randolph. Constable Ravina Sidhu shut him down, reminding him that gambling without a BC Lotteries Corporation permit was illegal, but she would let it go this time because she was late for the seniors residence, where she had volunteered to help with the bingo—the accumulated prize after five weeks unclaimed was approaching $600.

The final list of candidates was: Samson Spinner, Annabelle Bell-Atkinson, Finbar O'Toole, Sheila Martin, and Randolph Champion.

Silas said the four losers would take seats as the councillors.

Campaigning

While the Inlet echoed to the exaggerations, invention, and mudslinging that tended to inhabit all political campaigning, Jethro Wallace decided he would pay a visit from his Victoria home. He was curious about the contenders, suspecting that one of them at some future point might possibly challenge his own position.

Wallace was the Independent MLA for the Islands and some surrounding areas, the bulk of voters of which lived in Spinner's Inlet. He was a former accountant who had been charged with defrauding clients but was acquitted with the help of a Vancouver lawyer who had himself barely avoided censure by the law society over something concerning client expenses. He ran as an Independent after being rejected as a candidate by all parties in the last provincial election; he won the seat because none of the parties nominated anyone to challenge him.

The Liberals had held the seat previously, but their woman had been booed and unnerved on the ferry dock after having mistakenly assumed that Spinner's Inlet people would welcome a mandate appointing them British Columbia "tourism ambassadors." This would require them to wear badges and wave BC flags whenever the *Gulf Queen* docked and unloaded tourist groups, and no potential Liberal had generated the pluck to replace her. "In that place? You're joking," had been the repeated refrain.

The NDP had declined after one of their number had attempted a union membership drive among the Cedars pub staff and been escorted back to the ferry by the owner, Matthew Blacklock, who offered certain advice.

The Greens, given the uncertain tenor of things, chose discretion as the better part of valour.

Jethro Wallace happened to arrive in the Inlet as the latest edition of *The Tidal Times* came off the press, with a feature on profiles of the candidates. It was headlined "Personalities and Platforms."

Samson Spinner claimed (the aforementioned exaggeration) to have the highest measured IQ of all candidates but would not disclose it as he didn't believe in belittling others. Finbar O'Toole claimed to be descended from the legendary Irish king Brian Boru, and that subsequent forebears had constructed the Giant's Causeway (invention), and Randolph Champion marched in front of Gilbert's Groceries with a placard that claimed "capitalist and profiteer" Gilbert Chen was presenting day-old bread as fresh (mudslinging).

Sheila Martin said that Samson was at best deluded, Finbar was confusing legend with myth, and Randolph Champion was anyway half-baked.

Jethro decided that of that group only Sheila might have the right stuff, if she ever entered the provincial fray, and posed a threat. He asked her if she would like to have coffee, and said, "Another time, then," after she scowled, "What, with you?"

He was mystified by Annabelle Bell-Atkinson, who had declined any interviews and had made no statements, other than to drive around with her nephews, the geeks, in a spanking new convertible with the geeks holding up a banner carrying the cryptic message "CREAM WILL RISE," and with glaring ads on the door panels for the Victoria car-sales company that had loaned her the vehicle. It had mistakenly believed she was running for a seat in Ottawa (where they hoped to lobby against luxury-car sales taxes) rather than the mayor's chair in the Inlet. The geeks glared at Jethro when he threatened to approach, and he retreated.

Silas Cotswold had arranged an all-candidates meeting at the community hall. Jethro offered to emcee it. Cotswold, ever alert to any possibility of political advertising money, but also aware that Jethro's budget as the lone Independent in the legislature would barely let him rent a cellphone, said the MLA could do it. But he added that he wanted no partisan comments from Jethro and was reserving the right to step in if things became awkward. He gave Jethro a list of the five contenders with a brief bio on each.

The MLA received the obligatory derision due a politician, which he seemed to think was meant in good humour, when Silas introduced him, and there was uniform jeering as Jethro introduced the candidates one by one. The supporters of each were fairly balanced with opponents, and an equal amount of applause and boos ensued when platforms were presented.

Randolph Champion wore a tatty placard that said, "DOWN WITH THE ELITE. POWER TO THE PLEBS." An audience member asked him when he was going to get a job and pay taxes, like all the other plebs in the community. Randolph said that taxes were nothing but a further burden on the poor and that he would deal with *that* issue once he took office, and he shook a raised fist toward the interlocutor. The audience response was not something that could be thought of as approval.

Jethro stood and offered appreciative applause as Randolph plodded off the stage. He was alone in doing so.

Finbar O'Toole was next, and he opened with an ingratiating nod and smile before breaking into a mournful and reedy version of "Galway Bay," or at least the first verse, after which Jethro jumped up and asserted himself by loudly ruling Finbar out of order for inserting music into the debate. Silas Cotswold quietly advised Jethro to keep his opinions to himself as he had been instructed to do, adding, "If you call that music . . ." Then *he* ruled Finbar out of order.

Finbar offered an extravagantly knowing smile as he left the platform, and said, "How much longer do we Irish have to be picked on?"

"How much time y' got?" From a middle seat.

Jethro sniggered and received a hard stare from Silas.

Samson Spinner stepped forward and offered a pointed finger and a scowl at a voice from the back of the hall that said, "For mayor? *Really?*" The tone was rich in promising what its owner might know that others didn't, and Samson, despite his seeming confidence and his generally recognized reasonably good character, reacted like those of us who, when presented with the unexpected appearance of a police officer, rake frantically through recent events in a search for any law we might have flouted. His promises of competent and honest practice as mayor thus came off a bit shaky and he left to a low scatter of applause.

Annabelle Bell-Atkinson, who had remained seated in the audience, now rose and was escorted by the geeks to the platform, each of them waving a giant "Number One" foam glove. Annabelle struck a pose that made many who had known her aunt, the late self-appointed conscience of Spinner's Inlet, shudder. "Tomorrow is another day," she intoned.

"Margaret Mitchell. *Gone with the Wind*," Sheila Martin advised loudly from behind her.

"A new day," Annabelle continued.

"Celine Dion," Sheila murmured. "She's channelling them."

A flutter of audience laughter.

"Two roads . . ."

"God, now Frost. And you're sorry you can't travel both. We get it. But why don't you pick one, tell us where you're going on it, and take those two home." One of the geeks glowered at Sheila, then checked his watch.

The Bell-Atkinson trio left and Sheila took the podium.

"If those who have gone before me had been incumbents, we would question how they ever got elected. It certainly would not have been by people such as yourselves—aware, responsible, and wise. I know that those qualities will prevail when it comes to casting your ballot for mayor. Thank you." People looked about, searching for repositories of the values Sheila had credited to those present. They nodded and smiled knowingly to each other, then broke into applause as she left the stage.

Silas Cotswold escorted the MLA down to the ferry.

Wallace shook Silas's hand and said, "Finally I understand the kind of people who raised me to public office. I believe I can trust them to do it the next time around."

Silas nodded. "Yes, and good luck with that."

Two New Guys

The two young fellows chatted as they walked up the slope from the ferry dock. They stopped at the road, shook hands, and went their separate ways.

Willie Whittle watched them from the ticket booth as the taller one, with the black hair down to his shoulders, turned and waved. Willie gave him a thumbs-up. As he had walked off the ferry, he had stopped beside Willie and said, "Hi. I'm looking for a family called Spinner."

Willie grinned and looked up at the BC Ferries sign above the dock: "SPINNER'S INLET." "Looks like you came to the right place," he said. "Which one do you want? Samson, Rachel, or Jackson?"

"*Rachel*? She's still alive?"

"You might want to ask her." He considered that. "Or maybe not. What's your name?"

The young man told him, then said, "I'll try Samson."

"Up the hill, left onto the highway, about one kilometre, left again, road down toward the water, giant cedar on each side, big old house on a ridge. Can't miss it. Good luck."

Willie turned to the other young man, another stranger, about the same age as the first one, with a mop of fair hair. "Help *you*?" and soon gave him his directions, too. Willie made a mental note: Phone Silas at *The Tidal Times*. Item for the social column. A two-beer tip, surely.

The big old house, built with first-growth, rough-sawn timbers and rocks hauled up from the beach, sat like a sentinel above the inlet that the first Spinners had named more than a century and a half before.

A man in his sixties, wearing workboots, experienced jeans, a logger's shirt, and a perplexed look, studied a stone he was about to place on a low wall in need of fixing. The stone seemed considerably bigger than the hole waiting for it. He looked up as the stranger raised a hand and stopped close to him. "Hi. Mr. Spinner?"

Samson examined him. Then more closely. Looked away, then back. "Yes," he said. "Samson Spinner. Who are you?"

"Also."

"Meaning?"

"I'm also Samson Spinner."

Samson Senior placed the stone on the wall near the hole.

"I mean, that's my name," the young man offered. "I go by Sam." He frowned at the unrepaired wall. "I think we are distant cousins, or something." He seemed fixated on the wall, and the stone, and the hole where it was not going to fit.

Samson said, "Christ." Then, "I don't have any spare money."

Sam shrugged, dismissing the thought. He cocked his head, still staring at the wall.

Samson looked from Sam to his stonework. "Something wrong?"

"Well, I don't know about *wrong*, exactly . . ."

"But?"

"Well, it's just not how I would have gone about it." He swept an arm, taking in the whole length, about thirty feet, of the structure, which had an unevenness about it in several spots—dips and humps and such. "It's going to fall down, eventually."

"And what would you . . . ?"

"I'm a waller."

"A brickie, a bricklayer?"

"Waller."

"So, a kind of stonemason, then."

"No, brickies and stonemasons use mortar, like you've done in places. It'll crumble with these salt winds off the water, and . . ."

"It'll fall down?"

"Eventually."

"And if you built it?"

"As I said, I'm a waller. Like many of our—yours and mine—early family members. Dry-stone wallers. I'm from that branch. You lot are from the colliers, worked the pits on the west Cumberland coast. Ours worked on the fells. Then we left as well, went to Newfoundland." He shrugged, apparently in explanation. "We had an Irishman in the family—my great-great-uncle Patrick something. My aunt Lizzie has it all recorded, a family-tree thing. She goes on Find My Past, Ancestry, UK government records office, those kinds of things. I know quite a bit about us."

Samson looked at his unfinished job, wiped his hands on his pants. "Tell me about our wallers."

"Over a beer?"

Samson smiled. He went to the house and returned with two opened bottles of Sleeman's Honey Brown Lager.

They sat on the deck and Samson listened, and learned. . . . A trench four or five feet wide . . . two rows of footing stones on each side . . . space in between filled with heartening or little rock fragments . . . subsequent layers on top of the footings . . . each stone resting on two stones below . . . and finally the cam stones on top.

"And no mortar?"

Head shake. None.

Samson looked at his wall, considered the stones that lay about on the beach and the ones in the field behind the house. "Tell you what."

An hour later Rachel Spinner spun her veteran Dodge pickup into Samson's drive. She climbed out, carrying several three-ring binders.

Sam put down the stone he was holding and watched her as she advanced on him.

"Over here." Rachel pointed to a convenient log that had sat many Spinners, and opened one of the binders. Sam sat beside her, as directed, and listened and followed Rachel's finger running across pages of births, marriages, and deaths.

Rachel stopped, stabbed at an entry. "That's you," she said. She beckoned Samson over. "That's him. He's real. Look at this one. It's a copy of his great-great-grandfather's death certificate. Henry Spinner, died in Cockermouth, Cumberland. You know that's where Wordsworth was born, don't you? Cause of death, pneumonia. Occupation, waller."

"They worked winters on the fells," Sam Spinner said. "Freezing cold, pouring rain, they just kept at it."

Rachel nodded at Samson. "He's real, all right." She examined the corner of the new wall that Sam had started. "I hope you're paying him for that." To Sam, "Willie at the ferry said you had a lad with you. Is he another of us?"

"No, but he said like me he's here looking for a relative, an older one, forget which 'great' it was."

"What's this older relative's name?" Rachel asked.

"Svensen."

"Christ," Samson said.

Up . . . and Away

When seventeen-year-old Connie Wilson returned from a
trip to Victoria with her normally sandy-brown hair mostly
emerald green but with a few pink and purple streaks
and explained that that is what thespians do and that she
planned to become one, there were repercussions.

But first Connie's father, Charlie, had to be diverted
when he misheard the word "thespian" and started to
describe how he, as a liberal-minded modern parent,
would support his children no matter what they decided
they were, as he had had his own differences to overcome
as a youth. He did not clarify that his differences had been
mainly with authority and had resulted in two brief custo-

dial stays in the youth residential centre in Burnaby. It was explained to Charlie that Connie's choice was unrelated to sexual preference—although there were plenty of thespians who enjoy the varieties, as there were no doubt cowboys, mechanics, and cops—but rather it defined those who made their living on stage, screen, and radio, acting.

That was what Connie was setting as her goal, attending drama school. In a month's time there were auditions being held in Vancouver by the American Musical and Dramatic Academy (AMDA), on West 61st Street in New York City: musical theatre. Her dream. *The Wizard of Oz* . . . ruby slippers . . . Dorothy!

Connie was named in honour of her grandma, Margarita (Maggie) Consuela Pereyra-Mendez Wilson, a woman with an inclination to the dramatic, especially under stress, who, when Connie declared her passion, claimed that the urge to perform came from her side. This may have been borne out after she phoned 911 twice in two weeks, screaming for firefighters after Lennie got the toaster stuck on high. She got Constable Ravina Sidhu, who said, "Hello . . . emergency . . . No, I told you last time, Maggie, we don't have a fire department. There's just me. Should I bring my extinguisher down?"

Connie sounded like a songbird in the spring, and the kitchen floor at the Wilsons had a growing bare spot in front of the TV where she followed tap-dancing lessons on YouTube.

"This AMDA—how much?" Charlie asked.

Connie was aware that while her dad was a generous man, his pockets were never very deep, and especially lately, after the disappointing negotiations with Samson about the old blue truck at the Swede's funeral. "Bloody Spinners," Charlie had grunted.

But Connie was not discouraged. The immediate concern was cash to get to Vancouver and stay for the auditions, and she had a plan. All she needed was her dad's twelve-foot ladder, which she could repair with duct tape, a bucket, a sponge, and a chamois. She would wash windows.

Her first estimate, at the Inlet seniors complex, was rejected by the resident manager Jeremiah Bell. However, when Connie explained the purpose of her labours, Jeremiah, who had himself spent numerous hours as a background performer, or extra, on the old *X-Files* and a couple of other Vancouver-made shows, waiting in vain to be discovered, relented.

He advised her to start at the top row of windows so that any water and suds that drifted down to the lower windows would just help with the washing of them.

Connie propped the ladder against the wall so that the top rung, with the bucket attached by a wire hook, was adjacent to the first window on the left of the second floor, the highest. She climbed up, dipped the sponge into the bucket, and began spreading the good news.

Inside the complex, Hyacinth Jakes stepped out of the shower, lifted her robe off the hook, and turned at a squelchy sound from outside. As a ten-year-old girl in her home village in the Republic of Trinidad and Tobago, she and her junior class had once, in the interest of "introduction to theatre," been forced to watch a performance by a group of travelling players of the Victorian horror-melo-drama *The Face at the Window,* followed by *Maria Marten, or The Murder in the Red Barn.* She had been scared silly, and now Connie's face at the window, wide-eyed from shock as she felt the ladder's poorly repaired (duct tape) faulty right rail give way, and distorted through a wave of sudsy water, threw Hyacinth into serial-killer flashback mode.

Hyacinth screamed. Connie floated backward and down, still holding the ladder and shouting, "Sooooorrrrrry!" as she landed in Jeremiah Bell's newly prepared vegetable patch, where the soft soil cushioned her arrival.

Jeremiah, with visions of insurance claims dancing in his head, scooped Connie up, made sure she was all right, and paid her in cash from his pocket twice the amount they had agreed on for cleaning all of the windows, not half of one of them. He ran inside, grabbed the phone from Hyacinth, who was about to call for police, pointed out that she *really* needed to finish getting dressed, and promised her a nice cup of tea.

Charlie Wilson pulled into their driveway where Connie was busy working on the ladder. "How'd your first day go, kid?" he asked.

Connie finished putting the final wrap on a new course of duct tape, tapped it down, and looked up. "I was wondering," she said, "how many people might be needing their lawns mowed about now."

If Only . . .

Samson Spinner watched the passengers disembark from the *Gulf Queen*, jostling and laughing, on a dazzling Gulf Islands summer day. He wondered, once again, why he turned up every time the ferry came in on a summer weekend, disgorging happy, often festive, people, while he failed to dispel his own mood, which was a blend of illusory optimism and looming disappointment. And of course, he knew why.

He stared across at a group of four women of a certain age, close to his own, one of whom seemed to stare his way, nodded, smiled, and . . . my God! . . . could it be . . . ? But no, it wasn't. It never was, and no amount of wishful thinking was going to change that, was it?

If only . . . he wondered how many other people were tormented by that futile sentiment of . . . what was it? Regret? Remorse? Repentance? All of the above? What if I had . . . ? Or followed Annabelle Bell-Atkinson on election night and considered the other of the two diverging roads . . . the one that would have led to . . .

If only he had honoured the half-promises he had made to the widow, Thelma Spooner, when they were both young and she ran the post office. He smiled, once more remembering the time they had held a mock wedding. It had been a means of getting the provincial government road crews to save the old wedding tree they were supposed to cut down for a highway extension, and instead divide the new road into two to save the towering maple. They'd had champagne, and Samson had carved their names into a heart on the trunk, like kids do, prompting Thelma to say it was nice to have something in writing. And they had kissed, and the guests had applauded.

Those guests had long since stopped asking Samson if he had heard from Thelma, who, after accepting that there was not going to be a proposal unless she made it—and she was too damn proud, and had expected more of him, to do that—had been offered and had taken a supervisory job with Canada Post in Calgary.

She had left on a long weekend just like this one— sunny, warm, filled with promise for some. Since then she had sent him a couple of birthday cards with two kisses and love and best wishes from "always your friend, Thelma."

There had remained a slight connection, through Thelma's daughter, but then Heather had moved her riding club to Sidney on Vancouver Island, along with her two daughters and a son and her husband. Heather had always continued being civil to Samson, but with a distance about her. She had once remarked that she had been to Calgary and stayed with her mother, who remained single. Thelma, she said, appeared to concentrate her interests on her work at Canada Post, and the performances of the Calgary Flames. She said that her mother sent him her regards.

Samson had had on-and-off relationships, all of which finished as off, and had stayed unattached. Somehow none of them matched up to that first love, Thelma.

Should I . . . ? had been a recurring thought for Samson since she had left. Should I call her? Should I ask her if . . . ? But he hadn't, beyond a couple of Christmas cards wishing her seasonal joy and such, and those cards and good intentions had fallen by the way the last couple of years.

What if he had followed his first instincts and asked her to marry him, instead of letting doubts and uncertainty, and maybe a lack of confidence, dictate the future, which was now the present. What if?

"Samson."

He was snapped out of his reverie by a voice at his side. It was his recently arrived young relative and namesake, Sam Spinner from Newfoundland, who had just finished building a classic dry-stone wall on the old Spinner property, Samson's home. The wall had become a point of interest since Silas Cotswold had run a piece about it in *The Tidal Times*: "An Ancient Craft Come Home." Silas had even included graphics showing how the walls were constructed so that no matter the slope of the land, they remained horizontal. And he'd thrown in the information that the wallers of yore slyly included little runs that led rabbits to a surprise ending and supper for the labour force. The result had been a flow of Inlet people, and some from Salt Spring, to see the structure, and half a dozen—so far—orders for Sam to build similar walls.

"You meeting someone?"

Samson scanned the final few passengers leaving the *Queen*. "Not today," he replied.

"You looked like you were expecting somebody. They miss the boat, maybe?"

Somebody certainly did. "Maybe." Then, "What about you? You expecting somebody?"

Sam smiled and nodded at the last passenger, a young woman trundling a travelling case on wheels and making hard going of pulling the thing because one of the wheels had come adrift. He answered as both of them went to lend a hand.

"It's Cathy," he said. "She's a Sloan, from Marystown. Fishing family. We were unofficially engaged, and I wrote and asked her to come after Rachel said I could have that small cottage on her property—with caveats. She said I can stay in the cottage and Cathy will have one of the extra rooms in Rachel's house until we get properly engaged and then married. She said she's old-fashioned and that's the rule in her house."

"Not something many would want to dispute," Samson laughed.

He reached Cathy Sloan and hoisted her case while Sam hugged the girl and lifted her off her feet. They headed for Rachel's pickup, which had lately also become a waller's busy work truck.

After they got Cathy organized, and the girl and Rachel sat down for tea and talk, Sam said, "I tried to get her come with me at the start, but she wasn't sure, so far from home. She kept saying, 'But what if . . . ?' She never said as much, but she meant if it—we—didn't work out. What then? Because you never know, do you?"

Samson said, "No, you don't. But there's only one way to know for sure. And I can tell you that ignoring 'What if?' and getting on with it is a hell of a sight better than later on saying, 'If only . . .'"

Samson stopped his endless, fruitless checking of the *Gulf Queen* passengers . . . except for the occasional long summer weekend, when he happened to be at the wharf.

Ballots

The poll opened at nine o'clock, an hour later than promised in *The Tidal Times*, because Anwen Brannigan had lost the key to the Legion Hall, where voting was to happen.

"Mislaid," she said. "Not lost. And now I have it."

Anwen had been odd-jobbing and cleaning at the hall for a couple of years, since her brood had grown and fled for more promising climes. She tended to keep her own hours, and the fact that a mayor and council were to be decided (well, a mayor, with the also-rans becoming council by default) had not altered them.

She had addressed the complaint from Annabelle Bell-Atkinson, who was the first—and only, so far—one in line, that she had kept people waiting and disrupted their day. Anwen said, "There's nobody else here." And pointed about her at the absence of citizens waiting to vote. "I mean other than you, and those two [the geeks.] Anyway, I've got some dusting to do."

Annabelle asked, "Where are the ballot boxes?"

"Boxes?" Anwen said. "Where do you think we are, the United Nations? The box is where I put it." She pointed to the porch and an upturned cardboard item that had held cauliflowers for Gilbert's Groceries and had a scissored slot in the top. "You put your ballot in there." She added, "Gilbert supplied it free. Civic duty and all that."

"Where are the ballots?"

"On their way, apparently." She nodded toward a fast-approaching Silas Cotswold, who was on a health kick and thus on his bicycle, carrying a shoulder bag.

"Dusting," Anwen said, and she disappeared inside.

"Had a flat," Silas said as he dismounted. "Bloody cheap offshore products."

"Which nevertheless you bought," Annabelle noted. "As you did your computers and printers. Perhaps you could start a 'buy-Canadian' campaign. Make Canada great again."

"Again?"

Henry and Harvey started humming "O Canada."

Annabelle said, "Shut up."

"I'll get us set up." Silas parked his bike against the Legion wall. Inside, he dragged a six-foot folding table to the centre of the floor and placed a chair behind it with the cardboard ballot box, courtesy of Gilbert, on top.

"For the scrutineer," he remarked at the chair.

"Who would be . . . ?"

"Me." Aila Hanif had misjudged the time on her morning run and was a bit out of breath. "He"—indicating Silas—"thought that we needed an objective overseer."

Silas placed the ballots in a heap. He had printed the candidates' names alphabetically and had tried to create a square beside them for the X or check mark. His tech skills still required some refining and the squares had come up less than square. "They'll do," he said. "Just tell the voters to try to stay inside the lines."

Silas had a list of registered voters that MLA Jethro Wallace had obtained for him, which he laid beside the cauliflower box. The list was at least five years old and caused a problem when it was clear that Randolph Champion's name was missing.

That was because his lot had been in the Inlet only three years, and had never bothered to register. When this was pointed out to Randolph, and the suggestion made that as he was not a voter, it would be difficult for him to be mayor or to vote for himself or anyone else, he ranted and invoked the BC Human Rights Commission and various discriminatory legislative bodies that he could complain to.

He made such a noise about it that Silas simply added his name to the voters list and hoped fervently that Randolph would not become mayor. The fact that being among the four losers meant he would be on council anyway, Silas could deal with later, or someone else could.

While Aila got her breath back and waited with a sentry-at-the-gate demeanour to do her scrutineering and counting duty, Silas got the geeks to check off voters on arrival.

Sheila Martin complained that it was not really a secret ballot because there was no closed booth where voters could mark the thing. Silas, who was beginning to regret ever starting the process, murmured, "Bureaucrat," and received a wintry look, but smiled and had a geek find another cardboard box, cut open one end, and place it on a side table. "There you go," he said. "Just stick your head in there."

When no one was left in line to vote, Aila finished checking and approving the count. She handed the result to Silas, remarking, "Much easier than Kabul."

"Must be a real bugger there, then." He waved the paper at the remaining citizens. "And the winner—and our new, I mean first, mayor is . . ."

"Hold on!"

Anwen Brannigan appeared from the inner door, broom and dustpan in hand, and waving the latter. "Just hold on."

Silas glared, signalled to her to go away, and returned to his announcement. "The first mayor of Spinner's Inlet is . . ."

"I haven't bloody voted!" Anwen's broom was now at the present-arms position. Good job it wasn't a gun, Samson Spinner thought, as he watched things develop.

"Voting is closed." Silas tapped his wristwatch. "Twelve hours. You've had plenty of time to vote, like everyone else. The first mayor of Spinner's Inlet is . . ."

"My arse!" Anwen marched to the table, grabbed the sheet of paper from Silas's hand, folded it, and thrust it into her apron pocket. "The poll opened late, so it should close late. You arrived after I did and I was already late. Through no fault of mine," she added, although that could have been open to challenge. In fact, one of the geeks, fastidious for detail, was about to indulge himself by doing that, until Anwen shifted her broom position slightly and fixed a look on him.

"My democratic rights are being denied. I didn't raise seven kids in this community without a sniff of social assistance," here she pinned Randolph Champion to the spot with a telling glare, "to be told I'm denied a voice in its future. One vote can make a difference."

She smiled, sort of, at Silas, and commanded, "Give me a ballot—and then count them again."

He did, and she was right. Her vote tipped the scales and prevented a tie and a vote-off for the position of mayor of Spinner's Inlet.

With the result, Anwen received a warm hug from Sheila Martin, a thin and insincere smile from Annabelle Bell-Atkinson, and some ineffectual fist-shaking and grunting from the geeks.

Give It Up

The Clements twins climbed up onto the front deck at Samson's place, where he was taking a break from splitting alder for the living room fireplace. He poured the last drops of McEwan's Scotch Ale into his glass and finished off the rich, dark brew with a sigh, part contentment, part regret at the empty bottle, then a satisfying burp.

The kids were unusually quiet as they studied him. Something coming.

"Well?"

"What are you giving up, Samson?"

Alun posed the question. He and Jillian waited for Samson's answer, which was a puzzled, "Giving what up?"

"For *Lent*," sighed Jillian, as if to a slow learner. "Amber says we should make a sacrifice for forty days? Like God did?" Then, "What?"

"You're doing that thing again. That uptalk. Where you're incapable of speaking in simple declarative sentences. Every sentence ending in a question mark. You talk to people as if they're idiots. As if you're asking if they actually understand what you're saying. I mean, how is anyone to know when you expect an answer?"

Jillian rolled her eyes . . . this again. She dismissed it with a shrug.

Alun said, "Jesus. It was Jesus. Not his dad. And he didn't do it for Lent. He was out in the desert being tempted. Way before Easter was invented. People just use the forty days to see if you can last that long without going to the pub or having candy and stuff."

Alun was born a minute before midnight, Jillian a minute after. Alun took it upon himself to correct the kid whenever the chance arose.

"Moses did it as well, but not at the same time," added Jillian, who liked to fill in any glaring omissions by her brother. "And then there was all that rain for forty days and forty nights another time. Right, Samson?"

"Christ," Samson said. Then he deflected the original question. "You said 'Amber.' *Amber*? Don't you mean the Reverend Rawlings? We would never have called her father 'Randall.' Always Reverend. Respect, eh?"

"Randall?" Alun said. "Who would name anybody 'Randall'? That's funny." And he laughed.

"What is *Amber* giving up?" Samson asked.

"I think she said chocolate chip cookies," Jillian said.

Samson said, "I was right behind her in Gilbert's Groceries a week ago when she said she was done with cookies—chocolate or otherwise—because they were going straight to her hips. So, nice try, Amber. Happy Lent." He continued, "What about your mother—what's her sacrifice going to be?"

"Mom told our dad that she might give up Sunday morning lie-ins, if he didn't smarten up, but he said that was way too much to ask of anybody—or to, I think it was, *impose* on anybody—and she should think of something else."

Alun said, "And we know what that's all about, don't we? I mean the Sunday morning lie-ins. Oh, yeah."

Samson could swear he heard his eyeballs click. He managed a muffled, "Oh?" and hoped for a diversion, like the deck collapsing, or maybe a handy little tsunami.

"Of course," Jillian observed. "First one to get up from the lie-in has to make breakfast and take it back to bed for the other one. It's a rule."

"Ah, right," Samson murmured.

"Anyway, my mother said for you maybe beer," Jillian noted, with a nod to the empty bottle. "She figured it would do you good. Or wine. "

"She said *and* wine," Alun added. "Both. Together. At the same time."

Their mother, Julie, was principal of the elementary school.

"She would," Samson said.

"So?" Jillian cocked her head and waited.

"Well, first of all it's none of your mother's concern what I give up or don't."

Jillian's eyes widened at someone questioning her mother's word. And then she grinned at the thought. She said, "You should get going on it. It starts after Pancake Tuesday, which was yesterday, when you had all those pancakes at our house. My mom said it seemed like you hadn't eaten for about forty days, when she had to open another bottle of maple syrup. And that's when she started about Lent, and wondered if you be giving up anything. Grandma wondered the same thing, but said probably not because you don't have the self-discipline."

Grandma was Sheila Martin, retired secondary school teacher, recently elected the first mayor of Spinner's Inlet. Samson was one of the four by-default council members.

"She would," Samson said.

"And she said you would get crabby if you tried it."

"Crabb*ier*," Alun corrected her. "She said you're already crabby."

Jillian added, "Then Mom said Grandma should have said 'more crabby' not 'crabbier' because it didn't sound like proper English."

"She would know," Samson agreed.

Jillian said, "And to do Lent properly, you have to make sure you wash some of your friends' feet. Jesus did that for his apprentices. Washed them and dried them. They all wore those open sandals so it was probably easy to get dirt in them. He said they should do it for others, it would make them humble." She added, "Grandma said you probably don't know what that means, but you could still give it a try."

Alun said, "You can get humble as well if you give a lot of money away like the Queen does. We saw her doing that on TV last year. Some pensioners and poor people. I think they said it happens on Laundry Thursday."

"Maundy," Samson corrected.

"Whatever," Alun said. Then, "That's the day they had the last supper. Mom said you could come and have that at our place, if you like."

"My last supper?"

"She said you'll be ready for a drink by then."

"Tell your mother, and your grandma, that I appreciate their thoughtfulness and I will give the Lent thing serious consideration." Then, "But what about you two? What are you giving up?"

Alun smiled. "Grandma said we were to tell you that we are just the messengers. The rest is up to you."

"She would," Samson said.

Stop Sign

Sheila Martin smacked her gavel on the mayor's table.

Or, her "hammer thing" as Councillor Finbar O'Toole called it. It was an actual maple gavel that Sheila had found on eBay—placed there by a retired "President of . . . Local . . . union," the details of which had been mostly sanded off—for $9.75, which she had acquired for $7.75, hers being the only bid.

The table quivered on its four folding legs. Mayor Sheila had ordered a proper mayor's desk from a dealer in Victoria, but they had asked for a credit card number, in the name of the new Spinner's Inlet council, before they would ship it. After an emotional appeal to council to accept its fiduciary duty had been met with a restless silence, except for Randolph Champion humming tunelessly and Samson Spinner murmuring, "Nice try and good luck," she had eventually snapped that she would pay for the desk herself.

That may have still been on her mind when she demanded, "Order," although the only disruption to the current debate was Councillor Annabelle Bell-Atkinson. She was instructing one of her two geek nephews sitting in the public gallery (two picnic-table benches donated by Ali Hanif who had found four of them decomposing in a blackberry thicket, resurrected them, and applied a thick coat of leftover outdoor paint in a startling shade of royal blue) to go get her a coffee from Gilbert's Groceries across the street. "Double shot with two Splendas, and remind them that it's only two dollars at Timmies in town," she had whispered, though clearly not quietly enough to suit Sheila, who glared and pointed a warning finger at them. The geeks sniggered. Sheila frowned; it used to work when she was a secondary school teacher.

The debate concerned the proposed placement of a stop sign and/or a crosswalk near the seniors complex. The provincial government's highways department had been consulted, but an immediate return email had made it clear that those in Victoria who were familiar with Spinner's Inlet and its population were reluctant to get involved in anything there that might become controversial and worse—God forbid—require a decision.

"The minister has been advised of your concern and has forwarded the information to your Independent MLA,

Jethro Wallace, who, the minister is sure, will give it his earliest attention."

"Do it ourselves, then," Samson Spinner had concluded.

And thus the present council gathering, where contributions to the debate had been varied.

"The codgers should have enough sense at their age to be able take care of themselves if they get let out," said O'Toole, who added, "but if it has to be, I would give a good rate for all the painting and sign-building."

"Let the record show that he is all heart," said Samson.

Annabelle Bell-Atkinson noticed that Cameron Girard was busy with his pen. "Duty!" she declaimed, her eyes sweeping the public benches and the one chair with a cardboard label stating "PRESS ONLY" tacked to it, where Cameron sat, apparently paying attention. The public benches held the geeks, Erik Karlsson, the recent arrival to the Inlet, great-great-nephew of the late Swede, who was trying hard to get used to his new surroundings, and a couple from Mississippi.

When they had met the nosey Clements kids at the ferry dock, they had declared where they were from and asked if they needed to show their passports or were they still in America. They had then been treated to a chanted duet of the spelling drill—"Em-i-ess-ess-i-ess-ess-i-pee-pee-i"—of their home state, along with Jillian's dance version, and had escaped into the council meeting looking for directions as to how to get home.

"Duty to the needy and the old!" Annabelle continued. "Imagine when we have reached their stage in life and need to cross the road in safety. Who will be there for us?"

The coffee-run geek had just re-entered. He waved his free hand. "I will!" he promised, while his twin nodded approval and shot a thumbs-up toward his aunt.

Mayor Sheila slammed her gavel down. "Take your seat—this is *not* a public debate."

"Christ," Samson Spinner said.

Councillor Finbar O'Toole got the nod from Sheila to speak. But then she raised a palm—meaning hold on—crooked a finger at the coffee gofer, and when he approached her, apprehensive, she said, "Get me the same. I'll pay you later. And a doughnut." She smiled and the twin fled. "You were saying . . . ?" she said to Finbar.

Finbar's brow creased, then, "Yes, I was, but with all this stuff going on . . . give me a minute, Your Honour," and he sat down.

"She must be the judge," the American husband remarked. "I thought they wore wigs."

His wife asked, "Where's the perp?"

A few minutes earlier the Americans had had the significance of the forty-ninth parallel explained to them by Aila Hanif, who had started studying for her eventual citizenship test and had dropped in to experience the local version of democracy in action.

Finbar rose again. "I wish to make a movement."

"Not here, you don't," the mayor corrected him. "Try a motion."

"Right, then. I motion that we secede from a government that passes the buck, like the highways department, and join somewhere else that would be more helpful."

"We could inquire about that, if you like," the American wife offered. She seemed miffed when Sheila pointed a stern finger at her and made the zip-your-lip motion.

Dr. Timothy, who had just joined the meeting, said, "I tried that with the Turks and Caicos Islands years ago and they were willing—Turks, Caicos, and Spinner's Inlet, it would have been. We could have had Christmas and everything down there, but Ottawa turned it down and buggered it up. I'll give them another shout when Megan and I go down there again."

Mayor Sheila tasted her coffee. She frowned, beckoned the twin back up. "You forgot the Splenda," and handed him the mug. As he tottered away with it, his brother shook his head sadly and muttered, "You ask him to do *one* thing."

Sheila took a deep breath. "All in favour of the motion—Councillor O'Toole's, that is."

Both Americans raised their left hand while placing their right on their hearts. No one else moved.

The mayor's head drooped. "Motion is defeated," she sighed.

Samson thought she might be finding that running the new council was a different game from commanding a couple generations of students in the secondary school. And this was only the first council meeting. He was feeling relieved that he hadn't won.

Sheila hammered the table. "Meeting adjourned."

Cameron was just closing his notebook on a page that contained an especially lifelike image of the mayor, but with smoke issuing from her ears and flames—courtesy of a red Sharpie he carried and usually used to mark his golf balls—from her mouth.

Annabelle tried to get the reporter's attention, but Cameron sidestepped her and went to Karlsson.

For the next day's edition of *The Tidal Times*, Cameron wrote a profile of Karlsson under the heading "New Faces," in which the new Swede talked about the fascinating life history of his great-great-uncle, which he had discovered when he unearthed a will and a pile of almost legible notes at the bottom of a chest under a heap of used chainsaw files. The will had been witnessed by "Jimmy Plummer, Chief, First Nations Lands temporarily known as Spinner's Inlet."

In his regular news roundup, Cameron noted that the question of the stop sign and crosswalk at the seniors complex remained unresolved due to time constraints.

Barely There

"*What* optional?" Samson Spinner asked.

"Clothing, it says. Clothing optional. You can wear something, or not."

"On his beach?"

"He calls it au natural," young Jillian Clements replied. "He has it on a sign. With drawings. He says it's very common in Sweden."

"Says they are very open-minded there," her brother Alun added.

"Get in the pickup," Samson said.

Indeed, Erik Karlsson, the new Swede and great-great-nephew of the late Svensen, had posted a sign on his property line in front of the shack he had inherited from the Swede: "THIS BEACH IS CLOTHING OPTIONAL, AS OF THIS WEEKEND" In the bottom corner—"$5 PER PERSON." He had drawn two cartoon figures, one a man in an approximation of a Speedo, back to the viewer, the other a woman in her birthday gear, face on.

"Christ," Samson said.

Erik emerged from his cabin, grinning.

"What y'think, Samson, eh? You gonna take a dip, without . . . y'know?" and he mimed getting undressed. "Just like you came into the world, so should you swim."

Samson asked if Erik thought maybe he was in Vancouver, where "that stuff might be all right." And after a second added, "It's against the bylaws."

"Show me those," Karlsson said.

By the time Samson returned, after a fruitless search for anything resembling bylaws at the mayor's house, a couple fresh off the ferry was parading, sans cover, along the strip of sand and pebbles. They looked to be maybe in their fifties and with shapes that suggested their occupations away from the beach were of a sedentary nature.

"Flopping around like that, can't they see themselves?" remarked Rachel Spinner, who had followed Samson to the site. "Isn't there a law or something?"

Beside her, RCMP Constable Ravina Sidhu said, "Hmmm, well . . ."

Ravina had been alerted by both Samson—who had suggested an offence against public decency was underway—and by Erik Karlsson who had claimed that his constitutional rights to have whomever he wanted

64

to do whatever they wanted to on his beach, were under threat from Samson and "a gang," which now included the Clements kids, keen on having a second look, councillors Finbar O'Toole, Randolph Champion, and Annabelle Bell-Atkinson, and the geeks.

Behind this lot, on the track down to Karlsson's beach, trundled a growing trail of Inlet citizens who had somehow been alerted to the goings-on. Among these were Cameron Girard, with his digital camera gear, much of the population of the seniors centre, and the curious Aila and Ali Hanif.

"I think we would not have this kind of thing in Kabul," Ali explained to the reporter.

"You *think*?" his wife asked.

The nude pair seemed to be unaware of their audience. They were involved in a number of what seemed to be dance movements, their gazes focused first on the far horizon and then to the heavens, as their bodies came gradually closer together.

"Oh, oh," one of the geeks observed.

"Oh, boy," Randolph chuckled.

"Would you look at that, now!" Finbar said.

"Some people!" Rachel declared, and Finbar grunted, "Right you are," and kept staring.

"Close your eyes," Annabelle to the geeks. "And turn away."

The geeks obeyed, collided, and denounced one another's clumsiness.

Annabelle turned to Ravina. "Well?"

"Well, what?"

"What are you going to do? They're guilty of indecent exposure on a public beach."

"*Private* beach." Erik Karlsson, beside her.

Ravina was busy on her tablet. "Just a sec."

"And they're not exposed anymore." Erik pointed.

The couple was almost submerged, just their heads now visible. They were very close together as they bobbed along in a rhythm either of their own devising or to blend with that of the gently incoming tide.

"I think he just kissed her," Jillian Clements said.

"Or something," her brother suggested.

"If this catches on . . ." Samson warned, but to deaf ears.

Two of the seniors, Hyacinth Jakes and Willard Starling, who had recently formed an attachment, began edging toward the sand. Hyacinth pointed to Karlsson's board and asked if there was a seniors rate.

Rachel told them to grow up and go home.

By this time Julie Clements had arrived. She pointed at the children. "Home. Now." Then she glared at Samson and said, "Some example you are," and departed.

Samson called after her, "What did *I* do?" Then, "Christ."

Ravina looked up. "Here's something."

She beckoned to Erik, and when he reached her she indicated her tablet. "It's about property boundaries and briefly it says that your property extends to the high-tide mark. The land below that belongs to the provincial government, that is, the Crown."

She indicated the two nature lovers who were emerging from the waves.

"They are on Crown land. Your cabin is about five feet away from the high-tide mark. Nobody is going to want to go starkers in front of your place with you ogling them . . ."

Erik raised a hand to object. Ravina said, "Be quiet," then, "I hope that wasn't your intent, Mr. Karlsson, to charge people for taking their clothes off in front of your windows. There may be no law against it, but it seems a bit weird to me."

She looked around for confirmation and received nods. She glared at Cameron Girard, who suddenly found he had no use for his fancy camera.

Rachel picked up the pile of clothes and held them out to the approaching nudists. "You'll need these on the ferry," she said. She showed them her wristwatch. "And hurry or you're going to be late."

Samson took a small pry bar from his belt. "Help you with the sign, Erik."

Randolph on the Job

Randolph Champion was sensing changes in the air around his family.

The Toronto-born Randolph was an unrelenting supporter of the underdog, self-proclaimed member of the downtrodden, and persistent opponent of the controlling upper classes, which included just about everyone who did not share his views on paid labour—that it was an abuse of the lower classes, including himself, and thus to be avoided. (The fact that those in charge of the provincial welfare program, with its handy direct-deposit system to the Spinner's Inlet Community Credit Union comprised a paid workforce, he considered just and fitting.)

So the revelation that his thirteen-year-old son, Michael, had taken a job stacking shelves and sweeping up at Gilbert's Groceries after school and on weekends for five dollars an hour, was unsettling.

"Gilbert Chen is exploiting you," Randolph warned. "That is not even minimum wage."

"And I'm not old enough legally to be employed," Michael said, "So that makes us about even. Anyway, Constable Sidhu knows about it and she's not bothered. She comes in and asks me to move the freshest milk to the front from the back where Gilbert stacks it."

The next day Randolph appeared twice at busy times at the store and watched Michael work, which the boy seemed to manage without too much duress. In fact, both times Gilbert ordered the boy to take a break, go sit down for a bit, and gave him a couple of oatmeal-chocolate cookies and a bottle of juice of his choice from the cooler.

At home, Randolph told his wife, Storm, "I'm going to keep a watch on that situation."

Their other son, Billy, was also a cause for concern. At fifteen, he had taken to that most bourgeois of activities: golf. It had started with his being shown by industrious and profit-minded Inlet youth how to earn cash by hunting for golf balls in the rough and selling them back to players. He had then exceeded the usual practice of discovering and picking up abandoned balls, by stealthily following playing groups and finding "lost" balls before their owners could, thus increasing his inventory.

"Working for a faction of elite country club members," Randolph said. "Gin and tonics, white shoes, and tartan pants, and making serfs of innocent youth by requiring them to haul the weight of their overpriced equipment in severe heat at peasant rates . . ."

"We do not have a country club, Dad," Billy replied. "It's called Spinner's Inlet Golf Course. There's nothing elite about it because anybody can play if they can pay, including people like Samson Spinner, who wears shorts and runners, even with legs like his, and carries his own bag with five clubs. The only dress rules are no cut-offs and no T-shirts with rude messages. There's just a beer-and-wine licence. I think the only gin is in the flask carried by old Dr. Timothy, who says it's for medicinal purposes after the front nine. When I caddy I get paid twenty-five bucks for a four-hour round. I did two yesterday and got a ten-dollar tip on each."

Randolph's eyebrows moved. "Still," he said.

From selling found balls and caddying, Billy had earned enough to begin playing the game, renting a set of clubs donated to the facility by Annabelle Bell-Atkinson. She had bought them originally for the geeks to share in the hopes of getting them out of the house, but those two had proven mutually and extraordinarily incompetent. They had been asked to leave and stay away from the course following a sudden mood swing and an outburst of vulgarity that had alarmed a group of women golfers and required the posting of an embarrassing apology on the public notice board.

Billy had taken to the game and was showing potential, especially with help from two regular players: Cameron Girard—a relentlessly enthusiastic if marginally skilled golfer—and former Canadian Armed Forces Corporal Harry Dyson. As a youth Harry had played in the Rocky Mountain Amateur Golf Tour, and he was finding that coaching and playing alongside Billy Champion, and seeing the results, was helping him emerge from the gloom that his Kabul experience had brought him. He was back to a respectable six-handicap, and a brighter outlook on life.

One of Cameron's sports roundups mentioned that Billy's potential could one day take him to the riches-loaded Professional Golfers' Association (PGA) tour.

Randolph grunted and said, "We'll see about that!"

The next day he stood outside the gate to the golf course and, for reasons no one could quite discern, loudly quoted the late Groucho Marx's famous words: "I don't want to belong to any club that will accept me as a member."

Michael's announcement that Gilbert Chen had already promised him a fifty-cent-an-hour raise and could see him having management potential, seemed to be what spurred Kylie, his younger sister, into her own declaration that she was accepting a post as dishwasher, cash in hand, at the Cedars pub, where owner Matthew Blacklock had guaranteed that he would personally deliver her home safely after each shift and that it would not surprise him to see her become a full-fledged server soon.

Randolph's habitual protest concluded with, "You're thirteen! We'll see about this!"

And indeed, he visited the Cedars, where Matthew showed Kylie efficiently and happily taking care of the dishes in an immaculate, air-conditioned kitchen, where most of the work was handled by a massive and silent-running dishwasher that Kylie loaded, after having given the dishes a cursory dipping in a deep sink, and started by pressing a button.

"Nothing to it, Dad," the girl said.

"Humph," Randolph replied. Then he told Matthew, "*I* will pick her up, when she finishes."

"Thanks, Dad."

"To the victor," Blacklock murmured.

Storm was perusing a flyer from BC Ferries when Randolph entered the room. The paper was an ad for a part-time position at the Spinner's Inlet terminal—ticket selling and directing cars and so on. Storm, who had never held a job in their seventeen years of marriage, said, "This looks interesting. Coupla hours every other day, twenty-three bucks an hour . . ."

Randolph's lips were set to say, "We'll see about that," but he turned away. He had learned over their time together that his wife's parents had been something more than prescient when they chose her name.

Instead, he quietly took comfort in knowing that he had been saved from the demands of daily labour in order to be always available to deal with family issues when they arose.

Family Ties

For two decades Rachel Spinner had put great effort and endless hours into researching the history of the Spinner family. Some of it was fairly simple, starting with the family Bible begun by the original Samson Spinner and his wife, Maud.

Rachel had wondered what had happened before that pair's arrival and their naming of the Inlet. She had learned of the vast collection of family history stored by the Church of Jesus Christ of Latter-day Saints—the Mormons—and that a branch existed in Surrey, where she went and learned how to access their Family Search data. From there she had moved on to the websites of Find My

Past and Ancestry.com, and ordered copies of birth, marriage, and death certificates from the General Register Office in the United Kingdom.

From all of those sources she eventually had a family history going back as far as the early 1700s. This included one parish record showing that a certain family member was a "bastard child of . . ." and named a local farmer as the errant father, as they did in those earlier days, and a newspaper report from the mid-1880s of a distant female relative who had been fined ten shillings for the use of obscene language and lewd behaviour at the marketplace in the town of Whitehaven.

Those two she omitted (because who would be interested in such rubbish?) when proudly reproducing her findings for a feature in *The Tidal Times*, which she had persuaded owner-publisher-executive editor Silas Cotswold to run weekly, offering it to him at no cost. Silas had not taken much persuading. Like any owner of a print publication faced with vanishing advertising revenue in the face of the monster known as the internet, he grabbed at the chance of a freebie space-filler. Thus was born the feature "Our Families."

Soon after its appearance, an anonymous letter to the editor noted there was a lack of families other than "the damn Spinners" in the feature, and ended with, "What about the rest of us, the ordinary workers?"

Rachel ascribed this, correctly, to the self-appointed social activist Randolph Champion, though she thought he might have a point. She announced that henceforth, she would pick a name from the Inlet and, using her substantial research skills, begin tracing that family's history and would print the results weekly.

In fairness, because it was he who had implied that the Spinners had a monopoly, she thought she should begin with Randolph. This turned out to be less than a thundering success.

"Let me tell you right now," Randolph said, "before you even start your probing. You need to know that despite the scurrilous reports of the day, my great-great-uncle Ned was not guilty of those fraud charges he was convicted for. It was a set-up by the Wolverhampton constabulary and the damned judge who was biased against Ned because of the number of times he had appeared in his court, so if that's the kind of thing you're hoping to dig up . . ."

Rachel hoped for more fertile ground with Finbar O'Toole, given his claims of greatness in his forebears.

"I could tell you many stories," Finbar said. "Great stories—if only so many of our records had not been lost in the fire in the civil war Battle of Dublin in 1922. Stories of the real heroes of those times, heroes who will go unnamed because their names and their deeds were lost in that fire and could only be recalled in the memories of those now long dead. So you will have to go with what I have always been told of the O'Toole contributions to history."

Since he declined to say even which side the O'Tooles had supported during that civil war, Rachel thought it best she move on.

Annabelle Bell-Atkinson preened as Rachel accepted a cup of tea and prepared for a lengthy lecture beginning with how Annabelle had overcome many (unspecified) challenges as a child to rise in academic circles and acquire three degrees, all of it due to her genetic gifts from the Atkinson line, all of whom were . . .

Annabelle would have pursued this thread, but was distracted by her nephews, the geeks, erupting into a raucous argument that threatened to become physical over a computer chess match and could not be stilled.

Rachel said she would return another time.

"Do the Wilsons," Samson Spinner suggested, while Rachel frowned and fretted over Silas's deadline for the week's piece. "Surely it couldn't get much simpler than them, at least judging by Lennie. And Charlie."

Rachel thought the Wilson name was somewhat pedestrian, until she recalled that Lennie's wife Maggie, before her marriage, had had one of those foreign-sounding monikers and it might be interesting to delve into something different.

Maggie's pre-marriage name was Margarita Consuela Pereyra-Mendez.

"Spanish, then," Silas said helpfully. "I speak a bit of the lingo—foreign correspondent and all that, you know." He had once filed copy from Keflavik airport when his holiday flight was delayed by an ice storm "Let me help with this one."

Rachel agreed, as she needed to take a run to Salt Spring to stock up on supplies for her three setters. And what harm could it do anyway, with Silas being the old newshound and used to digging up stuff?

She stayed over with friends that night, and when she returned there was a letter on her porch bearing the return address of the law firm Ezekial Watson & Co., which actually meant that it was from Ezekial, who was also the "& Co." and who had recently moved from Burnaby and hung up his shingle next door to the Cedars pub in his plan for part-time early retirement.

The letter required Rachel to cease and desist from associating his client with such evil characters as Tomás de Torquemada, known for his penchant for torture and other horrors in the fifteenth century, and to "forthwith withdraw and retract the claims made in the most recent edition of *The Tidal Times* newspaper under the heading of 'Our Families.'"

It seemed that Silas had become confused while researching Maggie's Spanish antecedents, for whom there was little in the way of records, and his Spanish had become somewhat rusty, as had his knowledge of world history. He had assumed that the Spanish Inquisition had been some kind of public examination rewards board, and in order to speed up the process, and with his own deadline looming, had thought that connecting Maggie with that body would elevate her in the eyes of the community.

Maggie pinned the page from the *Times* along with the letter from Ezekial up on the three community notice boards, at the post office, Gilbert's Groceries, and outside the Cedars pub.

Rachel gave up on her quest to help others with their family histories. Silas filled the space by offering a "Buy and Sell" feature free to *Times* subscribers, or anyone else.

And Maggie Wilson wondered how she would handle the five hundred dollar bill for legal services rendered that she received from Ezekial Watson & Co.

The Grand Opening

The grand opening for Evelyn and Jackson Spinner's
B & B got off to a shaky start. From there it sped downhill.

First, the mayor of Vancouver phoned Evelyn
from Tsawwassen.

"What do you mean, you couldn't get on the ferry?"
Evelyn demanded. "You never bring your car so it's easy—
you walk to the ticket booth, pay, then walk aboard the
Queen. And walk off on this side. And you are my keynote
speaker, so . . ."

"Who else you got?" the mayor asked.

"Never mind that now. Anyway, how could you not get
on? I mean . . ."

"You know how they have that rule about ratio of crew to passengers and if one or the other number is out of whack, then the ship can't sail, no matter how much room there is left?"

"Go on."

"There's this group. They're hunting for a berry they say grows only in Spinner's Inlet. Apparently it produces a health drink like no other. There's a dozen of them, arrived on a bus, rushed aboard, the last to get on, and that was it. Too few crew for the number of passengers. I suggested adding a couple more crew but got told that would run into overtime and with contract negotiations going on, that was not going to happen. So . . ."

Evelyn had had the phone on speaker, which brought Samson Spinner into the conversation; he had come to see if any help was needed at the opening. "Maybe crowd control," he had suggested wittily.

"It's a myth," Samson explained. "The berry story, old as the hill itself." He was referring to Spinner's Mountain, all five hundred feet of it, where someone many years ago had claimed that the berry and its healthful content existed. "The story gets resurrected every so often, and you get a swarm of health freaks. They're wasting their time."

"They're buggering up my opening," Evelyn grumbled.

The mayor was not the only one with bad news.

The middle-aged couple who had arrived on the previous night's ferry for a week's stay was going to have to leave, following a phone call from Edmonton that had the wife weeping and the husband growling about "darned spoiled kids . . . never gonna grow up . . . in their bloody thirties." Evelyn felt she could not accept their offer to pay for the rest of the booked stay, them being so upset, and even made them ham sandwiches to take on the ferry, no charge.

"Maybe they'll come back sometime, you see."

Rachel Spinner had just arrived, also to oversee something. "And I need to talk to Jackson. Where is he?"

"Took a party to Salt Spring. Should have been back by now." Evelyn turned and pointed down to the marina, which was empty save for an American motor yacht and a local twelve-foot runabout waiting for gas. There was no sign of their water taxi, the *Chief JP*, which was usually tied up at the small dock south of the fuel pumps. "I think I'll need to talk to him, too." Evelyn said with a kind of tight smile. Then, "Anyone seen the Clements kids? I hired them for the event. They can get stuff ready and clean up after."

"I saw them at Gilbert's," Samson said. "Helping Finbar load the delivery van and looking like going with him. Maybe they forgot. Kids, eh?"

Others had arrived for the grand opening. Annabelle Bell-Atkinson with the geeks in tow stood by. Henry or Harvey raised a hand as if to speak but stopped when the new lawyer, Ezekial Watson, quipped, "Beware of geeks bearing gifts," and laughed at his weak pun. Ezekial had turned up with a raft of business cards, handing them out to everyone present. The cards read, "Personal injury, libel, and slander, et al." He moved through the gathering, muttering cryptically, "Just in case, y'know?"

A horn announced the arrival of the *Gulf Queen* at the dock, and the unloading began. The berry seekers came off like a commando unit, shoving people aside and flourishing maps as they headed up to the main highway and continued hurrying north.

A breathless phone call from an American couple who had booked the only ensuite room for a week advised they had been unable to board the *Gulf Queen* due to circumstances they didn't quite understand, which would never have been tolerated on the Washington State ferry system. They would not be arriving after all and hoped that their cancellation notice would be sufficient for a refund. Especially as they might return another time, when BC Ferries got itself sorted out.

Three Englishwomen strode off the ferry and collared Evelyn. "You look as if you'd know," one said. "We're looking for the area that's a little bit of Olde England." She waved a colourful brochure in Evelyn's face.

Constable Ravina Sidhu was close, having come to see if she could be of help with anything. She chuckled and tried a couple of sentences in her dad's Bradford accent. "Olde England," she explained to the trio, who seemed baffled, being from London.

"Don't you have anybody to arrest?" Evelyn suggested, and to the women, "You need Victoria. Different island." She would have added that she could recommend her husband's water-taxi service to deliver them, but there was still no Jackson in sight.

The owners of the two vessels waiting for fuel waved, and one of them hollered, "Anybody home?!"

Evelyn glared at Samson, who put down his wine-glass, headed to the dock, and started pumping.

The Englishwomen declined Evelyn's offer of space now available at the B & B, saying they did nothing but five-star, and would wait for the later ferry by way of Salt Spring. They bought three bottles of sparkling water and sat at a dining room table for the rest of the day. Evelyn did not feel that she could ask them to vacate the seats because they might be future patrons. Who knows?

By mid-afternoon the B & B remained empty. Complimentary bottles of wine had been breached and emptied by locals such as Randolph Champion and Charlie Wilson, who declared the event a smashing success and wished Evelyn well for the future.

Now the weather closed in, with heavy-bellied clouds filling in the western sky and delivering fat drops of rain that in seconds grew into a deluge, while the temperature plummeted. People crowded into the dining room, filling the space, but stopped talking when the community emergency siren began blaring.

At the same time, Samson's cellphone rang, as did those of all the Spinner's Inlet Search and Rescue team across the island. A group, apparently of hikers, on Spinner's Mountain was in trouble. One woman had fallen into a suddenly flash-flooded creek and broken a leg. Two others had been injured trying to haul the woman out and none of the crowd was dressed for the kind of conditions now in play.

"They never are," Samson grunted. "Christ."

Nor were any of them confident enough to begin the

trek down the mountain without help as darkness began to intrude.

Samson advised the room what was happening, and left.

A minute later Jackson Spinner rushed in, waving his cellphone. "Have to go," he said, giving Evelyn a quick hug. "Broke down in Ganges harbour earlier. Figured you'd be fine. How're things going?" as he left to join the rescue operation.

It was another two hours before the survivors and saviours limped in. Alun and Jillian Clements, who had become caught up in the excitement and followed the search and rescue, trailed in at the end, covered in mud, grass, and leaves, and went to wash up in one of the new and so far unchristened bathrooms.

Evelyn hurried to produce fresh coffee, served the berry hunters scones and soup, and poured a Scotch for Dr. Timothy. He had joined the fray and was checking for sprains and cuts and such. He drained the drink and said, "Well, no great harm done, after all." The broken leg had turned out to be a bad sprain. "Mainlanders," Timothy sniffed.

"What time is the ferry back?" The leader of the berry gang asked.

"End of the week, if you're lucky," Samson advised. "There's a strike and a lockout, just announced."

Mutterings among the berry fanciers.

Then the berry leader to Evelyn: "How many rooms do you have? For, like, a dozen, for a little while."

Evelyn smiled. "How many would you like?"

The New Doctor

Dr. Timothy was retiring. Finally. Not just talking about it again, but taking the last step. He announced that he had sold the practice to a newly minted doctor, whom he was going to introduce at a public meeting at the community hall, and that he and Megan would be leaving shortly.

"Sold" the practice was a bit of an overstatement. Medical practices all over BC had been sitting unsold for several years, with so many young physicians opting for jobs in walk-in clinics where they worked bankers' hours and could be fairly certain of paying off their student loans in a reasonable time. Dr. Timothy had never worked bankers' hours, or anything close to them.

"No one's going to replace him," Rachel Spinner had predicted. "Though they might take over his practice."

There was a standing-room-only turnout at the meeting because most of Spinner's Inlet had never known any doctor but Timothy. He had birthed and/or buried someone from almost every family. It was not uncommon for people to remain sick and wait for Dr. Timothy and Megan to return from their annual vacation to the Turks and Caicos Islands, rather than ride the *Gulf Queen* over to Salt Spring or Victoria and the tentative quality of care that one might find in either of those places.

"You never know where they might have come from," Charlie Wilson warned once. "Vancouver, anywhere."

Timothy and Megan walked onstage with a slight Asian girl and the three of them took seats. The audience murmured and whispered and looked offstage in expectation, and then back to Timothy, who finally raised a hand for silence and stepped to the microphone. It gave its usual initial shriek of protest until he kicked its base and succeeded in saying, "Testing, testing."

He said, "You all know me," which created a wave of laughter. "We have been through a lot together over the years. Most of you have been patients . . ." there was a lengthy pause as Timothy seemed to have to deal with a cough of sorts. He waved away an offer of a glass of water from Annabelle Bell-Atkinson, who had assumed a vague kind of supervising stance at the corner of the stage.

". . . mostly good times," Timothy was saying, "and it is time for me to say goodbye."

This evoked a quiet rumble of protest, which Timothy quelled with a raised arm and shake of the head. "And to welcome and introduce to you your new doctor," and he turned and gestured to the Asian girl sitting next to Megan. "Dr. Daisy Chen."

"Christ," Samson Spinner blurted. "Little Daisy!" He looked around and saw Gilbert Chen a couple of seats away offering a wide smile and two thumbs up.

Beside him, Charlie Wilson asked, "Who?"

"Daisy. Gilbert's granddaughter, from Surrey. Remember? She used to come and spend summers when Gilbert first moved here and bought the store from the Logans. She was about nine or so."

"And now she's what? Ten?" Charlie laughed.

". . . recently licensed to practise . . . and we are fortunate that she has chosen our community to begin her career. Please welcome . . ." and Dr. Daisy Chen got to her feet and went to stand beside Timothy, whose six-foot-one frame rose over her by almost a foot.

There was applause, hesitant at first but picking up when Dr. Timothy glared about the hall, challenging anyone daring to display less than unfettered enthusiasm.

"That's better," he grunted.

"Thank you," the new doctor said. "My office will be open as of eight o'clock tomorrow. And please, call me Daisy."

"And now school will break for recess," muttered Jackson Spinner who was standing with his wife, Evelyn, and next to his Aunt Rachel. "Is this really happening? What if I have to take my pants off when I go . . ."

"You'll have to grin and bare it," said the nearby Samson. "You know, as in . . ."

"Shut up."

As it happened, Jackson met Daisy sooner than he had expected to. Two days after her introduction, he was gassing up the water taxi at the marina and chatting to Cameron Girard, who was just nosing around looking for gossip, or even real stuff. A small sound of distress from the end of the marina nearest the B & B entrance, not unlike that of a lost kitten, was followed by a thump, and Cameron yelled, "Good God, Evelyn!" He started galloping along the wharf to where Evelyn Spinner lay sprawled, and still. "Call for help, Jackson!" Cameron ordered as he ran.

Jackson did so and soon also reached Evelyn's side. She was struggling to breathe, and continued to struggle as a panicking Jackson tried to lift her. "Evelyn? *Evelyn!*"

"CPR," Cameron snapped. "Chest compression. Try it! Turn her on her back!"

A patter of soft shoes on the decking. "Stand back," Daisy Chen said. "Let me have a look."

Jackson looked up and shook his head. "She needs . . ."

"STAND BACK!" Like a whip-crack. Then small but surprisingly strong hands pulled on Jackson's shoulders and he was out of the way and on his arse.

Evelyn was choking, trying to breathe.

Daisy began checking Evelyn's hands and bare arms.

"What the hell are you *doing*? It's her heart! She needs CPR!" Jackson shouted.

Daisy Chen waved him away and continued examining Evelyn's arms.

"Somebody get Doctor Tim . . ."

"Ah!" Daisy reached for her black leather bag, brought out a blue-and-green cylinder with a blue end and an orange one, with "needle end" printed on the orange. She slid the needle end through Evelyn's jeans and into her thigh, then watched. She smiled as Evelyn took a deep breath and almost immediately started breathing regularly. Within a few minutes Evelyn was on her feet, shaky but approaching normal again, and being held tightly by Jackson.

"Let her breathe," Daisy Chen said. "Then you can squeeze her if you like. It was a bee sting." She pointed to a small red mark on Evelyn's left wrist. "She is super-sensitive, allergic. She was going into anaphylactic shock. Her throat and mouth were swelling and preventing her breathing. Can be fatal."

She held up the cylinder. "EpiPen," she said. "Basically, adrenaline. Injects automatically into the muscle in the thigh. You'll need to get her one to carry with her so she or you or anyone else can do what I just did." She added, "However, get your taxi and we'll run her to Salt Spring for a hospital check. Just to be sure."

Cameron Girard was making notes. "Great story," he said. "Let me get a pic."

Daisy posed with the needle. "Make sure you spell my name properly," she said.

Dr. Timothy pulled up on his way to the ferry. Megan peered out from the passenger seat, and suitcases sat piled on the rear.

Timothy called from his opened window. "I saw

something was going on," he said. And to Jackson, "How're things?"

Jackson smiled, gave a little wave. "Things are fine, Doc. You're good to go."

A Twosome

The partnership that had developed between Tony Marconi and Howard Kennington-Longworth appeared to be in danger of breaking up.

Tony was a former longshoreman from Surrey, a burly, swaggering character and a weekender with a place at the south end. Born and raised on Vancouver's gritty east side, Tony affected the poise and charm of his namesake from the *Sopranos* TV series.

Howard Kennington-Longworth retired from his sales job at a men's clothing store and settled in the seniors complex about the same time Tony made his first appearance at the golf course, nearly three years before.

It was no secret that Howard had been separated from much of his savings in a notorious Ponzi scheme, and his closeness with a dollar was understood.

Each had signed up as a member. (Nothing fancy like some of the mainland courses, where a commitment to forty thousand dollars will get you onto a waiting list. Here, a hundred and fifty dollars a year gets you fourteen-day advance booking privileges, a ten percent discount on pro-shop equipment and bar drinks, and two dollars off green fees for anyone playing with a member.)

Howard and Tony were drawn as a twosome at a shotgun tournament their first week as members, and from there they just seemed to stick, showing up at the same time on Saturdays and Sundays, and Howard arranging to be available at other times when Tony's schedule was uncertain.

They had seemed at first to be an unlikely fit. Howard's demeanour had always been as composed and calm as Tony's had been uneven. Each seemed to have a quality that balanced the other: Howard had an unparalleled understanding of the etiquette of golf, and knowledge of its often-arcane and sometimes incomprehensible rules; Tony had a generosity of spirit and a wallet to match—his insistence that the next round was always his, and that he was simply rewarding Howard for the instruction he gave Tony, was accepted with grace. So the pairing had worked—until it didn't.

Tony was known as a really big hitter of the golf ball, at least as far as distance is concerned. Direction and accuracy were another story. That may have been behind the rift that developed between them.

It seemed that Sheila Martin was the only witness to the incident that changed things, as she explained to Samson Spinner while they played down the fifth fairway together. "I was playing behind them on number three. Tony hit one of his massive drives, about a mile to the right and into the big stand of firs with all the salal around them. He went in after the ball, shouted, 'Okay, I've got it,' and played a shot to about a foot from the pin. Howard stood and applauded, then he also hit to the green. He told Tony his putt was good and handed him the ball. Tony took his ball . . . and that's when Howard said, 'Uh, Tony, what ball were you playing off the tee?'

"Tony looked nonplussed for a second, gazed at the ball in his hand and said, 'A Top Flite.' Now as you know, Samson—as everybody knows, because he brags about it—Tony plays nothing but the best—and most expensive: Titleist."

"He does," Samson agreed.

Sheila said, "Then Howard asked, 'Not a Titleist?' Tony looked down at his ball, looked a bit flustered, but answered, 'That's the ball I hit out of the trees. So obviously I was hitting a Top Flite.'"

Samson grunted. "Oh-oh."

Under the rules of golf Tony would have been assessed a two-stroke penalty for hitting the wrong ball, and that would have been that.

"So, two strokes for hitting the wrong ball," Samson said. "And for—shall we say—making a mistake, about the ball he was playing?"

Some would have called Tony's actions cheating; there is no worse label in golf.

"They played two holes in total silence," Sheila continued. "Then suddenly Tony pulled out his cellphone, muttered something about an emergency, and left."

Samson said, "Christ! Tony was the one who insisted the course bring in a no-phones-at-any-time rule."

Versions of the story were passed around, and opinions were offered.

"You have to make allowances," Finbar O'Toole declared. "I mean . . ."

Finbar's opinion was given short shrift, knowing his propensity for managing to have a sudden elevation in his handicap in the weeks before any club tournament where money was a prize. ("Managing" being the word often knocked around.) Annabelle Bell-Atkinson, course treasurer, further devalued Finbar's contribution when she suggested he pay his overdue annual membership fee. "And last year's," she added.

As Sheila was the leader of the women's golf group, her description of the event was listened to carefully, though she warned each time, "Remember that I was some distance away, so I cannot swear to every detail."

Sheila's title used to be ladies club captain, before Dr. Daisy Chen took over the practice of the departed Dr. Timothy. Daisy turned out to be a very useful nine handicap. And something of a progressive. "I think 'women' is more realistic than 'ladies'—I mean, how many of those do we really have among us!—and more inclusive. And surely 'group' rather than the exclusive connotations of 'club.'

Also, 'captain' tends to have an authoritarian ring, don't we think?" (Daisy would know; she acquired her post-grad and medical qualifications courtesy of the Canadian Armed Forces, in which she finished up herself wearing that rank's three pips on her shoulder board.) Daisy's surge of egalitarianism won the day.

Sheila did not offer an opinion on the matter of Tony and Howard and the golf balls. She simply said, "We must all respect the rules of golf."

At the same time, she was not about to let the matter fester. And it bothered her that the situation was creating an ugly mood, both in the clubhouse and on the course.

People had started taking sides, some claiming that they had heard from Tony that the incident had been exaggerated and that he had genuinely mistaken a ball lying under a leaf for his own, and that Howard had rudely refused to accept an explanation and an apology.

Tony had made no such claim, but when Howard declined to offer his own version, knowing it would just add to the divisions, his silence was taken by some to confirm the false rumour.

Both men dropped their names from the senior men's team that played other local clubs once a month. This meant a scramble for replacements and, when that failed, complaints from the other clubs about their schedules being messed about.

Both Tony and Howard were suffering from the event more than anyone should, which was remarked on by Daisy Chen, among others. Tony had almost stopped showing up, and if he did, it would be around twilight, when he would tee off on his own, a lonely, bulky figure with drooping shoulders, which, given that posture is critical, did nothing for his golf swing, as was attested to by his observations when balls flew in myriad directions.

Howard continued playing but avoided Tony's tee times—and Tony. If they happened to be in the parking lot at the same time, each would let his gaze move to the ground and go his own way. Both stopped going to the bar.

"They're both in danger of becoming depressed," Daisy diagnosed.

They're not alone, Sheila thought, and decided that they'd all had enough.

"It's only a bloody game when all is said and done," she told Samson.

She advised Tony and Howard that in her role as head of the course discipline committee (until then, nobody had known there was such a body), she demanded a meeting with them in the bar. She ordered the drinks. A glass of his favourite Okanagan red blend for Tony, a pint of Granville Island pale ale for Howard, and a large chardonnay for herself.

"You're making everybody miserable," she told them. "And we're going to stop it."

Rarely had two faces shown such a blend of curiosity and, clearly, relief.

Sheila placed a sleeve of balls on the table in front of each of them. She handed a blue Sharpie to Tony, a red one to Howard. "Mark them," she said. "Every one, and all your others. It's too easy to make a mistake if you don't. I have you booked as a twosome for ten o'clock Saturday morning."

As the drinks were delivered, she said, "Tony's round, this one." And in the words of golf announcers everywhere, she added, "Play away, gentlemen." And of golfers to each other, "Play well."

Not in This Stocking

It was Christmas Eve and the Spinner clan was gathered at Rachel's place.

Rachel listened as young Jillian Clements declared that Finbar O'Toole had told his kids they were going to get nothing but coal in their stockings this year.

"Hah!" Rachel said. She shared a smile with Samson, her nephew, who nodded and indicated, let the kid continue, for now.

"Liam forgot to feed the chickens for two days in a row. Siobhan left the pasture gate open again and the pony got out and they're still looking for it. And little Paddy told his dad to eff-off."

Everyone busied themselves with their Christmas drinks.

"So that's it. Coal in their stocking. No Santa," Jillian concluded.

Her brother Alun snorted at 'Santa,' and Jillian said, "Shut up, you." Then, "The same as the prime minister, at least." She referred to the morning's headlines in which the black mineral gift had been proposed for the PM by the leader of the opposition in Ottawa.

Rachel stirred. "They should all think themselves blessed," she said. "Including that fool back east."

Samson considered that most anyone holding the highest office, regardless of party, would have been thus labelled by his aunt, but he knew better than to note this.

"What do you mean, 'blessed'?" Jillian asked.

"Well," Rachel began. Samson grinned and waited for another generation of Spinners to be re-educated on the common misapprehension.

"Let me tell you about coal," Rachel continued. "Samson Spinner, your . . ."

"Greatgreatgreatgreatgrandad," rattled off Alun.

Rachel recounted the greats in her head. "Good lad," she said.

"Was a coal miner," Jillian instructed. "Back in England. In the county of Cumberland, where life was hard. So they came here and he never went down the pits again."

Rachel was pleased. "That's right. But he and his wife, Maud . . ."

"Our greatgreatgreatgreat . . ."

"Right, Jillian. Now let me continue."

Everybody settled, including the dozen or so who had heard the lesson before, but never tired of it. (Or if they did, they never showed it.)

"They never forgot that the mines had given them a living, hard as it had been. The mines had made it possible for them to get themselves here and buy land on which to raise a family. If they hadn't done that, none of us would be here today."

She paused, sipped on her single malt. "Let me tell you about coal."

Try to stop her, Samson thought.

"Samson and Maud left a lot of people behind who kept working in the mines. Some of the Spinners became active in the miners' union, which eventually improved their working conditions and their lives," she nodded. "But that's another story. At the time that Samson and Maud arrived here, other colliers from their home and the rest of Britain came out to a place not far from here . . ."

"Nanaimo!" Alun declared.

"You're starting to get it," Rachel said, with a smile. "We have a bit to go yet."

"Mom's taking us there next week for the Boxing Week sales. I need new shoes," Jillian said.

Rachel continued. "There's a story—a real one—about how there came to be coal mines at Nanaimo."

Samson always enjoyed this one.

"A chief one of the Nanaimo First Nations—the Snuneymuxw in their own language—had gone by canoe to Victoria to see the blacksmith and get his rifle repaired. He noticed that the forge was fuelled by coal and asked the smith where the coal came from. The other side of the world, the smith replied, and it took at least three months to get here. The Snuneymuxw man laughed and said they had lots of the black stuff on the beaches where he lived. The smith laughed, too, and said, 'Yeah, right.'"

"Or words to that effect," Jillian said.

"Shut up, you," her brother said. "You're spoiling it."

Rachel carried on. "The Snuneymuxw man went home, but a few months later he returned, with his canoe filled with coal."

"And, 'There you go, buddy!'" Alun said. "Or words to that effect."

Rachel explained. "The chief became known as 'Coal Tyee.' There is a bronze bust memorial of him near the lighthouse. That was the start of an industry that built the city of Nanaimo and brought people from all over the world, not just Britain, to work the pits. The pits provided a better living. Prosperity, even."

Jillian said, "Okay, but what does this have to do with stockings and Christmas?"

"Well, your great-great-great-great grandfather, Samson, brought with him a custom . . ."

"First footing!" Triumphant, from Alun.

"On New Year's Eve in coal-mining villages, you have to have a tall, dark-haired person be the first to enter the house, and you give them a large glass of whisky for good wishes in the New Year . . ."

"I knew that!" Jillian.

"But there's still the most important part," Rachel said. "What does the first footer carry into the house?"

"A lump of coal!" several voices echoed.

"Exactly. A lump of coal—and not because anyone had been bad, but because coal was the source of all their livelihood. A suggestion that it would continue to be just that. A sign of prosperity. Good wishes and hope for the future."

Nods and smiles all around.

Mostly.

"But burning coal causes global warming," Jillian said. "Which is going to drown us all."

"Or possibly fry us," Samson shrugged. "Who knows?"

Jillian made a face. "I've been reading about coal. Even Queen Elizabeth was 'grieved and annoyed' by the smell of coal smoke."

"What about Philip?" Samson asked. "What did he think?"

"Elizabeth the *First*. Sheesh . . ."

Samson said, "In the 1660s the College of Physicians in London advocated the burning of coal to combat the bubonic plague."

Jillian snorted. "How do *you* know?"

"Read it in that book of yours. What's it called again?"

"*Coal.*"

"That's the one."

A week later the same gathering raised their glasses and sang "Auld Lang Syne" as midnight approached, and shouted "Happy New Year!" as the clock chimed midnight.

A banging on the door quieted things. Rachel went to answer it.

Edward Plummer, the youngest of Evelyn's brothers, six-foot-two with raven hair, stood grinning. He winked at Alun across the room.

"Happy New Year," he said. He reached out and placed a lump of coal in Rachel's hand.

Samson said, "Where . . . ?" Rachel embraced Edward. "That's how it's done," she said. She led him to the food and drinks and poured him a large Scotch.

Two days later, across the water, a volunteer at the Nanaimo Museum gift shop studied the display of lumps of coal with their $1.99 price tags. She said to a colleague, "I'm sure there was another piece at the end of that row."

Con Job?

Rachel held the phone away from her for a moment.

The woman's voice, a youngish one, had shaken her.

"I'm looking for a Rachel Spinner who was engaged to my great-uncle during the Second World War."

Rachel's heart sped.

She looked at a framed photograph on the wall over her fireplace. A young Rachel in a blue uniform—skirt, tunic, and cap—with the two thin stripes of a second officer in the British Air Transport Auxiliary, and a pilot's wings. One of the hundreds of young women who ferried every type of new and repaired military aircraft between assembly plants, transatlantic delivery points, and active service squadrons and airfields across the UK. Beside Rachel, a slim young man in Royal Air Force blues with flying officer's rings on his sleeves. Jack Thomas.

"Hello . . . do I have the right . . . ?

"What was his name?"

"Jack Thomas," the young voice replied. "My father was his nephew."

Jack. Rachel's Jack. A Welsh farm boy who had answered the call as soon as war was declared. In a pub, she laughed when Jack brought her a pint of bitter instead of the gin and orange she had requested. "More for your money," he'd said, with that smile. The smile she fell for— and forever stayed in love with.

"Where was he stationed?" Rachel asked.

"Biggin Hill. Near London."

Rachel's eyes welled. Memories. All she had, along with a picture on the wall.

"Where are you?" Rachel asked.

"Vancouver."

"What's your name?"

"Sally. Sally Thomas." There was a wait of a few seconds, then, "I really need some help."

Rachel had known little of Jack's family in the brief time they had been given, and in the chaos of war had met none of them. She did know that she would not be the first senior to be called by someone they had never met, claiming to have a family connection and requiring help.

"What kind of help?"

"Well, like, some money . . . ?"

Of course.

The young woman hurried on. "My dad always said that if I ever got into trouble while I was travelling, he was sure I could call you for help. His name is Philip. He was Jack's nephew."

"How did you know where I live?"

"It was in the free paper, the one in the boxes. It said, 'Reprinted from *The Tidal Times*.' It was quite a coincidence, eh?"

Quite.

"So, I wonder if you could see your way . . . ?"

It would have been the profile.

Times owner Silas Cotswold had been running a series titled "Prominent Personality Profiles" and Rachel had agreed, after much beseeching, to talk with the young reporter Cameron Girard who was writing the series. (Cameron had told all his subjects that Silas had an arrangement with other newspapers that paid him a modest fee to run any of his features they found attractive.)

Cameron had dubbed Rachel "Matriarch of the Clan."

"Like 'Monarch of the Glen,'" Samson had quipped, but not to Rachel. "Without the antlers."

Cameron had produced several other profiles before managing to corral Rachel, and had failed with other possible subjects. Finbar O'Toole had demanded a hundred dollars for an interview. "The British tabloids all pay for exclusives." Constable Ravina Sidhu demurred on the grounds a profile might "out" her and expose any undercover work she might undertake in the Inlet. And the Bell-Atkinson geeks had both begun to talk at the same time, and the resulting chaos and confusion had persuaded Cameron to leave them be.

Rachel had been surprised at how many details the young charmer had taken from their conversation over tea and raspberry scones, and she was impressed by the piece he had written. And now it had impressed at least one other, and was being put to use. The profile had been packed with detail about Rachel and her war experiences.

"I think we should meet," Rachel said. "Where are you staying in Vancouver? I could catch the ferry, or you could come . . ."

"No, you don't have to do that . . . and I'm not going to be here long enough. I just need a little help . . ."

"I would like to meet you. Jack was very important to me."

"Yes, I know about that. It was terrible."

"How was Jack known among his pilot friends? What did they call him?"

"Taffy."

As any Welshman was called, and as Rachel had heard over and over in the pubs that she and Jack visited with his flier mates: "Hey, Taffy, it's your bloody round!"

Rachel chuckled.

"So . . . ?"

"How much do you need?"

"Enough to get me back home. To Toronto. Soon as I can. I've had some problems."

Rachel waited. Memories arose. Walks down country lanes, grassy banks with wild primroses, daffodils, holding hands, a kiss, and another . . . and then, nothing, just another name on a long, sad list.

She sighed. Then, "I will help you."

"*Thank* you!" And quickly, "I'm near a Western Union office, on Hastings Street."

The Downtown Eastside. Of course. Dealers, users, sidewalk overdose deaths.

"Two things though."

"What?"

"I cannot do it until tomorrow, until our credit union opens."

"But the internet . . ."

"Tomorrow."

Finally, "All right."

"And the second thing."

"What?"

"Promise me that you will do what you say—go home, to your family. They will be missing you." She added, "Not everyone gets a second chance."

She put the phone down. Then she went online and checked the price of one-way airline tickets to Toronto. Then she called Constable Ravina Sidhu.

The next morning Rachel was at the credit union when it opened, as was Ravina.

It had not taken Ravina long.

"That is her real name, Sally Thomas. And she is from Toronto."

Rachel nodded, and waited.

"But she is a pro. She's been scamming seniors across the country and skipping just ahead of the police.

She's an expert at online researching, a real whiz apparently. She was kicked out of the University of Waterloo when she did her first job on the head of her computer studies department. She said she was just experimenting. Her specialty is looking for obituaries, and building a family connection from there. She can start way back, old newspapers, stuff like that."

Rachel smiled. It was one of the avenues her own genealogy searches took her down and had done for years. It took her a long time to learn it. Sally Thomas, it seemed, was a quick learner.

"What do you want me to do?" Ravina asked and frowned and shook her head at Rachel's reply.

Rachel walked home, made herself some herbal tea, and smiled as she studied the photographs of Jack and herself.

Ravina returned a couple of hours later. "My Vancouver Police Department buddy checked. Sally Thomas cashed a transfer for four hundred bucks."

"Right."

"She took a cab marked 'Airport Service.'" Ravina poured herself a cup of tea. "Maybe it'll work out . . ."

Rachel looked at Jack's photo. Was the smile a bit broader in the afternoon light?

"Maybe it will."

Burns Night

The Tidal Times had made the declaration a month ahead
that there would be a Grand Burns Night celebration at
the community hall, "in memory of the Bard of Ayrshire,
and everything Scottish."

Silas Cotswold himself had designed the front page,
which was replete with thistles, lions, and a blue-on-white
St. Andrew's cross—a saltire—in each top corner. The
page had been reproduced on posters that Silas hung
around the community, most of which had been removed
by unknown hands as soon as they were fastened up.
Silas denounced the vandals in a half-page editorial and
said the guilty would get their comeuppance.

The Bell-Atkinson geeks, who were the vandals, carried a smug look. They had recently returned from a two-week trip to Great Britain and had seen some old posters exhorting the citizenry to "Keep Britain Tidy," which they had removed in their belief that the posters themselves were anything but tidy—as were, they decided, Silas's Burns Night posters.

The night started with Sheila Martin delivering Burns's "Address to the Haggis," the words of which, for anyone not raised five hundred miles north of Carlisle, are largely incomprehensible. The chief reason the audience stayed with her to the last line—"But, if ye wish her gratefu' prayer, Gie her a haggis"—was that many of them had gone through her English classes at the high school and remained acutely aware of the consequences of inattention.

Silas next read from the program. "And now an open mic performance on a Scottish theme. Volunteers . . . anyone?"

Samson Spinner muttered, "Ah, Christ," as Finbar O'Toole rushed to the stage and unfolded a printed sheet before grasping the microphone.

"A limerick," Finbar said. "An original one," and launched into:

"There was a young lass frae Dundee
Who desperately needed a pee.
She stopped at the vicar's . . ."

Julie Clements raised her eyebrows at Alun and Jillian, but the kids ignored her and, along with the three O'Toole siblings, joyfully assisted with the rest of it:

"Then lowered her knickers,
And said, 'Just pretend you don't see!'"

Sheila Martin, trying and failing to make a stern face, told Julie, her daughter, "You have to keep them away from that O'Toole house."

"Shut up, Mom!" Julie snapped.

Always ready with a line from the actual Bard, Sheila replied, "Sharper than a serpent's tooth . . ."

Alun won a coin toss with Jillian for who should do the thistle piece. He jumped onstage and took the microphone.

"The thistle," he declared. "Would you like to hear about the Scottish thistle?"

He carried on, undaunted by the silence. "The thistle you might think is just an old prickly pointy thing. But that's the point." He paused, grinned. "Point, get it?" And after a further void, "Anyway, the prickles came in useful way back when some attackers were creeping up on Scottish soldiers who were sleeping. The enemy took their shoes off so the Scots wouldn't hear them—but they stepped on thistles, and that was them done for. The Scots jumped out of bed and killed them. I think they were English," he added. "And they haven't been back since."

At this point a side door crashed open and Scott McConville, the Inlet's veterinarian, marched in holding aloft a platter with what purported to be the evening's pièce de résistance, a haggis, though this steaming, amorphous lump bore little resemblance to the real thing, mostly because Scott had dumped the ingredients into a bowl shaped to create Christmas plum puddings. Scott claimed Highland blood back to Robert the Bruce. Rachel Spinner, skilled genealogist, had been tempted to press him for details but decided to let sleeping dogs lie, given that Scott was caregiver to her kennel of beloved Irish setters.

Jillian asked, "What's actually in a haggis?" Samson explained, "You take a sheep's stomach, stuff it with its heart, lungs, liver, and whatnots like oatmeal and salt, and cook it. It's a bit like a meat loaf, but basically, it's boiled guts–offal."

Jillian performed the gagging thing with her forefinger, and sound effects.

It is traditional at Robbie Burns nights for the haggis to be piped in, but invitations to the Greater Victoria Police Pipe Band, the Vancouver Firefighters Pipes and Drums, and the internationally famous Simon Fraser University Pipe Band had all been graciously declined.

"They have a reputation to protect, after all," opined Annabelle Bell-Atkinson, whose offer to cook the haggis had been also graciously declined by Cotswold, who believed she got her name in the paper enough as it was.

Instead of a pipe band, Scott was led in by RCMP Constable Sammy Quan from the Salt Spring detachment playing "Scotland the Brave" on his bugle, freshly polished for the occasion and decorated with a tartan tassel. Sammy said that was the McQuan plaid of a branch of the family that had its roots in a Hong Kong-based quartermaster sergeant-major of the Queen's Own Cameron Highlanders, who had passed through the crown colony at some point.

Annabelle Bell-Atkinson took to the stage and, with a signal to the geeks who started hammering on the piano, she roared into the "Skye Boat Song": "Speed, bonnie boat, like a bird on the wing, Onward! the sailors cry . . ." She followed with a lecture about Bonnie Prince Charlie and his Jacobites and their defeat at the hands of the despicable Duke of Cumberland at the Battle of Culloden, in which she managed to suggest that early Bell-Atkinsons were involved, though she failed to clarify which side they supported.

Sheila Martin remarked that Annabelle's affection for her two corgis suggested a strong affiliation for the establishment, so her family probably did not support the Young Pretender.

A voice from the back corner of the hall announced, "Scottish dancing!" In no time the place was awhirl with flying kilts and bouncing sporrans, exposing sets of knees and other items that would have been better left covered.

Randolph Champion's sudden contribution was to shout, "Sword dancing," and start to wave around a claymore he had ordered from Amazon for the occasion. The thing was five feet long and weighed about five pounds, in US measures, and, given Randolph's condition courtesy of the early and short-lived free bar, could have caused decapitations. However, Constable Ravina Sidhu jumped in, handcuffed him, and stuck him in a corner with a warning to "Stay!"

The microphone crackled, and on the stage Hyacinth Jakes demanded attention. She announced that residents at the seniors complex had been rehearsing "the Scottish play" and were about to present some selections, if everybody would pay attention.

Someone asked where the other two witches were.

Hyacinth said she would portray Lady Macbeth. "Who, as you will know, was sleepwalking, and declaims, 'Out, damned spot! Out, I say!'" She stopped, looked down at her hand, and sputtered, "Out, goddammit!"

Her recent swain, Willard Starling, rushed onstage to cover for her, but the retired heavy equipment operator became confused as he spread out his hands. "Is this a digger I see before me?"

There was noise from a corner where Erik Karlsson was arguing that the haggis had been actually first created by Vikings on their way to invade Britain and in need of sustenance for the long journey in their longboats. "They brought sheep with them just for that," he explained. "They knew that the sheep's stomach would be the perfect container and . . ."

Jillian shouted, "Hey, look," and pointed to where the haggis, apparently forgotten, had fallen from its platter due to the dancing's reverberations, rolled under the piano stool, and was being attended to by the aforementioned corgis.

"Good dogs," Samson muttered.

The evening was beginning to deteriorate and could have gone in any direction until the youth factor stepped in, in the form of Connie Wilson, Charlie's daughter, who had just received word that her application for the American Musical and Dramatic Academy in New York City had been accepted for the fall. Her singing especially had convinced the audition judges.

Connie took the microphone and began, a cappella,

"O my Luve is like a red, red rose
That's newly sprung in June . . ."

Charlie was beaming with pride as the crowd began humming along. But when she reached the final verse,

"And fare thee weel, my only luve!
And fare thee weel, awhile! . . ."

he noticed that she was gazing in a particular direction. He followed the look and found himself staring at the adoring eyes of Liam O'Toole, Finbar's oldest and of an age with Connie. Finbar also made the connection. To Charlie's dismay, he winked at him and gave a thumbs-up.

With alarming thoughts of such future nuptials in his head, Charlie decided then and there that Connie was going to New York, no matter what, and wondered if perhaps there might be an earlier, spring semester.

The day after the event, Silas Cotswold offered fifty

percent off annual subscriptions (fifty dollars) to *The Tidal Times* for anyone joining *The Tidal Times* Spinner's Inlet Robbie Burns Society by the end of the month. Membership in the society was recently set at a hundred dollars per annum.

On the Run

It was Jack Steele's idea. The Kiwi exchange teacher had read another report about the increasing obesity epidemic in Canada and most of the rest of the developed world, and decided that Spinner's Inlet should set an example. There would be a community "Run for Your Life": five kilometres for kids, ten kilometres for "others." The kids would be given an earlier start, to clear the course.

He first went to Silas Cotswold and asked that the event be publicized in *The Tidal Times*.

"Like an ad, you mean?" Silas asked, and showed Jack his rates sheet.

When Jack demurred and said it would be a gesture to benefit the community, Silas said he was not a charity, but he would, if Jack preferred, give it some space on the condition that it would be known as "The Grand *Tidal Times* Annual Community Run for Your Life, Sponsored by *The Tidal Times*."

"There hasn't been one before," Jack pointed out.

Silas offered to add "First" before "Annual" and to give free entry for any new subscribers to the *Times*.

"It's already free. We're hardly going to charge people for getting fit."

Silas said that may be how things are done in the Antipodes, but perhaps Jack should recognize an act of generosity, a gift horse if you like, when it appears, especially to a foreigner, and if he couldn't, well . . .

Jack muttered something about "higher authorities," went home, and dispatched an email to the premier of British Columbia with a copy to the Inlet's MLA, Jethro Wallace, explaining his plan and noting that so far, local support had been less than hearty.

Someone in the premier's office replied immediately, wishing Jack the very best of luck, and asking him, "How long have you actually lived in Spinner's Inlet?" With a rolling-on-the-floor-laughing emoji.

Jethro Wallace's executive assistant responded soon afterward, explaining that as much as the MLA would have loved to join in and/or assist, a recent attack of gout made even slow dancing beyond him, ". . . so it is with regret . . ."

Jack recalled what a teacher friend from the mainland had said about how in the village of Fort Langley, notices of their annual run were printed and hand-delivered to the doorsteps of all those along the route, advising them of an early start that might, without a heads-up, alarm normally late risers and high-strung mutts.

He chose in his case to co-opt the Clements kids to go door to door and verbally advise citizens of the happening. When Jillian asked how much it was worth, he lectured her on community spirit and sent them on their way.

The two were particularly well received at the seniors residence, where Hyacinth Jakes immediately got onto the recently installed intercom early warning alarm system and shattered the afternoon quiet with a blaring announcement that "A new day is coming!" This brought into play Hyacinth's sometime-beau Willard Starling, who stepped from his apartment waving his Bible and shouting, "Hallelujah!"

Hyacinth told him to go back to bed.

She told Alun and Jillian that she would guarantee a good cheering section from the old folks, and volunteered to have the lawn at the residence set up as the third and final refreshment and check-in site.

Alun asked Jack if pets were allowed to compete in the race, saying their new pup, a rescue spaniel-border collie cross from the SPCA in Victoria, would benefit from the exercise, and that its two breeds were known for both stamina and speed. They had named him Marathon.

Jack shrugged but corrected them, saying that just as at school now, competition was not the point; rather, it was all about participation and inclusion. "If you call it a race, everyone will try to be first and heaven knows where that might lead."

"Possibly a sense of achievement," Samson Spinner provided, happening to overhear the discussion. "Although we would not want to declare a winner and leave everyone else suffering a diminished sense of self-esteem, would we?"

Jack wondered, not for the first time, what retro part of this new country he had landed up in. He snapped that there would be no blue ribbons at any event that he was organizing.

Samson responded, "Right. Give them white ones, saying 'I was there.' Christ," he added.

Jack had things to organize.

He needed to set up three refreshment points along the course, with bottled water available. He had alarming memories of the film from Vancouver's 1954 British Empire and Commonwealth Games that he had watched in teacher training at the University of Auckland. The British marathoner Jim Peters had presented a nightmare state of affairs as he reached the stadium in first place, seventeen minutes ahead of the next runner and ten minutes ahead of the record, but, seriously dehydrated, staggered and collapsed repeatedly, and failed to finish. After covering just two hundred metres in eleven minutes, he was stretchered away and never raced again. "I was lucky not to have died that day," he later said.

Jack determined that as well as reducing the risk of fatalities, the refreshment stops would provide each runner with a numbered disk—one, two, and three—on a string to be hung around the neck and checked at the end, thus assuring that every runner had actually run the full course. He cut the disks himself, from several lengths of half-inch dowel, and centre-drilled them for a string. He numbered them for the different stages.

Meanwhile, Samson wrote a letter to the editor, decrying the growing wimpiness of society, especially as demonstrated in Jack's refusal to call the run a race.

The issue heated up in more letters, and it rankled Silas, who wrote increasingly volatile editorials favouring the competitive element. He had been a decent miler at school in Chilliwack, winning the Fraser Valley Secondary School event one memorable year, and still had the cup to prove it. As an anonymous ("Notes from Boz") school sports correspondent for the Vancouver *Province*, he had also reported on the event, lavishing praise on the winner in terms that elevated the eyebrows of the usually blasé sports editor.

The memories of his track triumph glowed brighter as the pro and con letters poured in to *The Tidal Times*, and spurred Silas into unusually charitable action. He announced there would be five hundred dollars in winnings—two hundred and fifty each for the kids and the "others" category—the money to be donated to a good cause of each winner's choice.

Jack Steele said he might cancel the event, but Samson called him a poor loser and a disgrace to the Commonwealth, whose games were replete with winners and *losers*, and things went ahead.

The start, before a large and noisy crowd, went well. Constable Ravina Sidhu commanded the entrants into an orderly line. ("Tallest on the left, shortest on the right.

Atten*shun!*" Then, "Stand easy.") And Dr. Daisy Chen checked the pulses of each of the runners and gave them an encouraging hug and a sound pat on the back.

Ravina examined the sleek and astonishingly complex GPS systems being worn by the Bell-Atkinson geeks and decided there was no rule to prevent their use. It didn't matter, as the pair got into a positioning squabble at the intersection of Keswick Road and Derwent Way, and went their separate routes. They were not seen again until late in the evening.

Finbar O'Toole joined the race late, but in front. He joined partway through, suddenly appearing from behind the refreshment table at the final stop, next to the seniors complex, breathing dramatically hard and chugging from one of the free bottles of water. He grabbed one of the final-stop stringed disks, added it to the two already around his neck, the designs of which he had copied from a detailed diagram in the *Times,* and ran on to the finish line, apparently the first to be done, panting after his run and with clasped hands raised in triumph, just like in the Olympics.

The Clements kids were close behind him. They were well ahead of the remaining runners, having been dragged at speed by Marathon who, on daily jaunts, had become used to the sustaining bowl of water and snacks left out by Hyacinth.

Constable Ravina was in charge of collecting the disks. She checked Finbar's three, offered a hand in congratulation, and nodded to Dr. Daisy, who came forward. Daisy smiled at Finbar, took his arm, and turned him around so his back was to her.

There was no sign on Finbar's neck of the red maple leaf that she had applied to the nape of all starters with a small, rubber, pre-inked stamp.

"Arrest him?" Ravina queried.

"No. Just tell him that if he's going to wear shorts, he'll look better with matching socks."

The Clements and Marathon were declared the winners of the kids group.

The "others" group was being led by the two recent arrivals to the Inlet—the young Sam Spinner and Erik Karlsson. They were shoulder to shoulder, pushing hard, lengthening their already-long strides, eyes on the finishing tape about two hundred metres ahead, and the two hundred and fifty dollar prize.

Behind them, Jack Steele loped easily along, smiling at the pair battling ahead, arms flailing, heads flopping around, panting. It looked like they were drowning on dry land. Jack laughed. Then he didn't. One of this convulsive pair was going to take the honours?

Images of legendary New Zealand runners leaped to mind: Sir Peter Snell . . . Sir Murray Halberg . . . Sir Jack Walker.

Sir Peter seemed to look at him: *Well?* And faded away, humming "God Defend New Zealand."

Jack flew past the struggling pair and broke the tape.

Alun and Jillian said that their two hundred and fifty dollars was going to the Victoria SPCA, ASAP.

Jack said he would match his winning amount for a worthy cause, as he shoved the cheque and the blue ribbon into his shorts pocket.

Two weeks later the Spinner's Inlet Secondary School boys rugby sevens team appeared at a mainland tournament dressed in replica kit of the New Zealand All Blacks. They faced the competition, then formed the famous wedge and moved into the grunting and snarling *haka*—a ceremonial dance or challenge in Māori culture, performed by New Zealand and many other rugby teams, which Jack had learned from his Māori grandfather. It involves vigorous, threatening movements and stamping of the feet. Jack's team's performance sent several small children running to their mothers.

Jack paraded the winners' trophy all around the *Gulf Queen* on the way home.

Ravina and Grace

Constable Ravina Sidhu waved at Grace as her friend made her way up among a stream of passengers from the ferry.

Three high-school boys Ravina knew were behind Grace, and the idiot of the trio, Gerry something or other, started imitating the young woman's awkward stride—until Ravina fixed him with a look that would have etched marble. Gerry tried a phony ingratiating smile as the group came abreast of Ravina, but the Mountie wasn't having any of it. He lowered his head and went on.

"Doesn't matter," Grace Kin said as she saw the interaction. "Not anymore."

Ravina wondered, and worried about, just *what* didn't matter anymore. Sounded like more than mockery from another fool.

The crash had happened off the exit from Highway 1 to McCallum Road in Abbotsford, when an old pickup with a driver over the drink limit had T-boned the Kin family's Ford Taurus. The pickup driver was awaiting trial on several charges while his defence lawyer conjured up every trick he knew to delay court action.

The Kin family, meanwhile, mourned the death of Jung-jin, husband and father. Grace's left leg had been severed at the knee. Her mother, Ji-woo, and younger brother, Tae, were in hospital for three months recovering from numerous injuries.

Ravina had been onto the ferry and up the Trans-Canada at top speed when she'd heard the names of the crash victims. Grace was her closest friend and confidante as a woman and had been since they attended Abbotsford Senior Secondary School through to graduation.

The injury to Grace had stopped short the professional golf career she had been dedicated to—earning a place on the Ladies Professional Golf Association (LPGA) tour—as were thousands of other young women in high schools, colleges, and universities across North America, and most of the rest of the world. Grace had begun and shaped her game at Ledgeview Golf and Country Club, the site known for producing such golfers as Ray Stewart and Adam Hadwin, both champions on the Professional Golfers' Association (PGA) Tour, the men's version of the LPGA Tour.

Ravina had caddied for and cheered Grace on through qualifying and mini-tours, and she had wept for her and with her after the crash. She had tried humour as a therapy when the local newspaper reported that the War Amps had stepped in to help Grace with a prosthetic leg.

"'*Stepped in!*'" she had groaned. "Can you believe they said that?" Grace had managed a smile. Ravina had continued, "I mean, how lame was that?" Then, "Oh, no! Tell me I didn't just say *lame!*"

Grace said, "LOL," and laughed.

But there was no laughter in Grace now, Ravina thought. She knew that Grace had stubbornly refused the therapist who suggested that she use a cane while trying to manage the prosthesis, and her struggle was clear. The sympathetic nods and smiles that came her way seemed only to deepen a dark mood. The Grace that Ravina knew and loved was *not* a "doesn't matter anymore" person.

After the crash, while her mother and brother were recovering, Grace had taken charge of the family's small herb farm—"and try our organic honey!"—with the help of two cousins from Richmond who ran a similar operation there. The business was surviving.

Ravina had had her own share of finger pointing as a child, growing up where skin colour had still been a subject for some for derision. She had listened to and absorbed her father's suggestion that she "Get over it. Those few don't matter. They're idiots."

Grace was staying for a week with Ravina. The next day she accompanied Ravina to a weekly drop-in, every-body-welcome session at the high school. It was open subjects: anything to do with the community, especially the youth in the community. Characters like Gerry and his buddies usually looked in, and especially now with pot being legal, to see what the local cop was going to go on about.

Ravina introduced Grace to the group of a dozen or so. "One of the best women golfers this country has ever seen."

"*Was*, maybe." Possibly Gerry.

Ravina pointed a finger at Gerry and a couple of his followers. "With me." She led them outside and pointed them into her minivan.

When they arrived at the driving range—an unfenced hayfield next to the golf course, with a raggedy mesh net about two hundred and forty yards from the practice mats to stop any golf balls that managed to get that far—Jack Steele was busy, and making heavy weather of it, trying to put into practice the suggestions and tips being offered by Harry Dyson, the former soldier and almost-member of the Hanif family. Jack's swing was no threat to the mesh net. He had been explaining to Harry that he thought his main problem was with his takeaway. Harry was an excellent golfer and had won the club championship with ease ever since he had arrived in the Inlet. His expression seemed to suggest that Jack's takeaway problem was his very least.

Grace Kin watched Jack's efforts and grimaced. To Ravina it seemed like either pity or wonder. Maybe both.

Ravina looked at Grace and cocked an eyebrow. Grace shook her head, negative. Ravina decided on shock tactics. "To quote the old English proverb my father always used . . ."

"From Bradford, right?"

"Don't be an arsehole. The world does not spin around you."

"Revolve?"

"Get a club."

Grace sighed, then shrugged. "Whatever."

On the practice mat, Harry said, "Jack—and I say this as a friend—you're not getting it. You're going to have to start paying for lessons."

"But, mate, there isn't a . . ."

"Sorry, my boy. I can't take you any further."

The discussion halted when, "'Scuse me. Borrow your driver for a sec?" Jack Steele looked down at the diminutive Grace Kin, who smiled politely up at him. Way up.

"Well," as he fondled his brand new Cobra King F9 Speedback that had set him back $449.50. "Watch it, new jumbo grips . . ." He glanced down at Grace's hands, which, for a small woman, seemed especially well developed. "Go on, then. And be careful. It's my only driver, now . . ." This alluded to the fact that earlier, in a moment of incompetence-induced rage, he had deconstructed a new Ping G400 Max Driver ($649) against the sharp edge of one of the ten-by-ten posts that supported the range's new retractable canopy. This addition had enabled the club to advertise the range as "all weather"—part of a general improvement drive directed by a select committee.

There had been fundraising whist drives, bingo nights (with a permit), and putting contests on the member-volunteer-built new green behind the clubhouse. The geeks had won three successive putting contests and there was some conjecture concerning the connection between a hand-held gadget and the unerring roll of their ball to the cup, but the healthy result of the growing numbers turning up to pay to watch had discouraged any questions.

The improvement committee comprised Dr. Daisy Chen, her uncle Gilbert, Annabelle Bell-Atkinson, and Matthew Blacklock, owner of the Cedars pub. Matthew had played his part by adding ten percent to a dozen drinks and snacks on his menu and placing a logo of a soaring golf ball beside each item. Gilbert, who was a non-playing (tried once and walked away, shaking his head) social member was hauling all his shop's returned deposit items to the bottle and electronics recycling depot. The operation had recently been opened near the ferry dock by a young couple new to the community. Gilbert donated the cash to the golf club's improvement fund.

Blacklock was an erratic golfer, with a handicap sliding between thirteen and twenty-four. On the stillest of days, following another errant shot, he would shake his head as though mystified, spit-wet a finger, and raise it to test whichever non-existent breeze might be culpable. He now watched Grace Kin, with a contemplative expression.

Grace took a couple of rehearsal swings. ("Don't call them practice," her father had always urged. "Make them real.")

She swung softly and the scarred and bruised, yellow driving-range ball sailed off and snuggled into the mesh net.

"Christ," observed Samson Spinner, who had joined the group, which was expanding as others left the clubhouse to watch. "Here," he said, handing Grace one of his shiny new Callaway Chrome Soft balls straight out of the package.

Studies have proven that driving-range balls—battered and beaten by repeated use from hackers such as Jack Steele—will lose from ten to twenty percent in distance compared with regular balls. Grace placed the new ball on the tee, laid into it with a rhythm and power rarely—no, never before—seen at the Spinner's Inlet Golf Course. The ball was last seen flying about twenty feet higher than, and a very long way past, the mesh net and over a stand of aged alder trees.

"Jeezers!" cried Gerry. Then to Ravina, "I'm really sorry, Rav . . . er . . . Miss . . . er . . . Constable."

"How's your iron play?" Samson asked Grace.

She picked a couple of clubs from Jack's golf bag and showed them how her iron play was. "And of course, anyone can putt," she said.

A month later Dr. Daisy, her own game having gone south, waited her turn at the new rehearsal tees, where solid, three-quarter-inch-plywood panels had been installed between the mats, a blessing for anyone practising next to the likes of Jack Steele, or Samson Spinner for that matter.

The Kiwi was improving under the tutelage of the improved Spinner's Inlet Golf Course's recently hired—

and first—golf professional, Grace Kin. She was taking a week off to shoot a TV commercial in Monterey for the internationally known golf-equipment manufacturer Play-Fair Golf, whose scouts had accepted pressing invitations to "Check out this Abbotsford kid." Grace was to be the company's TV and magazine presence, introducing its new lines of footwear, clubs, and bags.

Constable Ravina Sidhu was taking some owed leave to make the trip with her best friend, and maybe to caddy a couple of rounds at Pebble Beach after the shoot.

Post Office Blues

The front-page headline in *The Tidal Times* was only slightly smaller than would have served the declaration of another world war: "POST OFFICE DEEMED DOOMED!"

Beneath it, in a slightly less strident font: "We have been speaking to an undisclosed but usually impeccable source and we believe that Canada Post is about to announce the change of our beloved post office from a public operation to a private one."

After running the story, *The Tidal Times*' owner/publisher, Silas Cotswold, handed Cameron Girard a clumsily written note. "There's a rumour that Canada Post is going to close down our post office and put it out to private tender."

"Where's this from?" Cameron asked.

"Just a source."

"So, anonymous then." And probably nothing to it. But he knew better than to suggest that to Silas, after the last time.

Silas had advised him, "I learned long ago, Cameron, that the secret in this business is making something out of nothing. My first city editor was told by a new reporter that there was no story in a particular assignment, that nothing was happening. The city editor said, '*Why* was there nothing happening? *Who* was it not happening to? *Where* and *when* was it not happening?' All the basic Ws."

"But . . ."

"Get a comment, Cameron. Do a streeter," Silas said.

A streeter, of course.

Cameron hated them. Stop anyone and everyone you can and ask them their opinion about an issue, watch them preen as you note their answer and ask, "Will I be in the paper tomorrow?" And, "Are you going to take my picture." And, "My name's an odd spelling so . . ." And fairly often, "Slow day, eh? Bugger off."

Silas said, "Get to Sarah Flynn at the post office. She's the supervisor."

Cameron frowned. "She's the only person who works there."

"Are you still here?" Silas asked.

"What *about* this impeccable source, though? That's going to raise questions."

"We never give up a source. Say you would go to jail before you would disclose that."

"But I don't know . . ."

"Go, before the TV people get to her."

"The ferry has been and gone. They'd have to come in by boat or chopper. Do you think the story is that big?"

"Big? Look at the size of that headline!"

Cameron stopped Samson Spinner and started, "Mr. Spinner, I don't know whether you've heard . . ."

"I'm in a hurry, Cameron. I have some mail to collect and somebody said there's a problem at the post office. Always something, isn't there, eh? One bloody thing after another. Just like life." And was gone.

Hyacinth Jakes interrupted Cameron as he started to pose the question. "Yes, I know, the post office. Well, let me tell you, young fellow, things have not been the same since they stopped calling it the Royal Mail, back in the late 1960s. They may have left her face on a stamp, but . . ." and she shook her finger at him, as if assigning guilt, and stalked off.

Late '60s? Wounds deep and lasting.

But there came just the person.

The ageless Danny Sakiyama. Canada Post/Postes Canada (CP) shoulder flashes, dark-blue CP-logo ball cap, crossover harness on the shoulders holding a delivery bag on each side, all-seasons blue shorts, rugby socks in orange and black—a salute to his beloved BC Lions—and North Face hikers. How old was Danny now? Getting on, because there were those stories about him being one of the oldest posties in the country after he had declined the offer of a retirement party when he hit seventy. "I'll let you know when I'm ready to go." And that was a while back, so if anyone would have a valid opinion . . .

"Danny . . ."

"Don't ask me, I just work for them. But let me tell you . . ." And he did. ". . . resulting for people like me in more forced overtime, more stress . . . and then there's the letters to Santa Claus . . ."

"That's volunteer, isn't it?"

"But you know, it's all about the personal touch."

"Thanks, Danny."

"And that's the difference between us and the private operators: the personal. If this change happens, when you reach the counter, it'll be, 'Oh, hello, that'll be five bucks or whatever and there's the door and have a nice day.' None of the special treatment like we give, like Sarah at our post office gives."

"Such as?"

"Well, whenever young Todd Shackleton gets another publisher's rejection letter—about one a week— she's there to tell him another one has arrived and to encourage him to persist, a most important word to an unpublished writer."

"How does she know it's a rejection slip? What if an acceptance arrived?"

"Oh, she'd be on the phone lickety-split to tell him to get his ass down and check out the advance."

"But how does she know?"

"Did you know that George Orwell's *Animal Farm* was rejected by fourteen publishers? And Margaret Mitch-ell had to have twenty goes with *Gone With the Wind*? I

tell ya, life for an unpublished writer can be a real bugger."
(Cameron thought, Hello . . . *My Life With a Mailbag* by
Danny Sakiyama?)

"Yes, but how *does* she know what's . . ."

"The personal touch, like I said. A different lot—the
private—would just leave him to fret. So let's hope the
story isn't true." And he was gone, mailbags swinging.

Randolph Champion was at the head of a queue
outside the post office with one of his protest placards,
which read "Down with . . ." and the rest was so far blank.

"Multi-purpose," he explained to Cameron, who
hadn't asked.

Dr. Daisy Chen appeared and grabbed Cameron by
the hand. "I do not like the sound of what's happening,
Cameron. It'll be the same people who want to privatize
our health services. Dollars for diagnoses, I call it. Tell
them . . . well, think of something rude and tell them that,
from me. And you can quote me."

"Let me get a picture, Doctor."

"Left profile, if you would," Daisy said.

There was chatter in the lineup.

Maggie Wilson. "They're going to move it private, into
a drugstore like they do on the mainland."

Other voices: "We don't have a drugstore . . ." And,
"Salt Spring does. Maybe . . . Oh, gawd . . . What about
Sarah? What will happen to her? None of a new lot will
look after people like she does. She ran after me with my
glasses and library book the other day, when I left them,
all the way to the pub." And, "Always has the kettle boiling,
for a cup of tea, or whatever . . ."

Cameron asked, "Where is Sarah? I need to get her opinion on all of this."

"You'll have to wait." Rachel Spinner, with a handful of envelopes. She pointed to an elegantly handwritten notice taped to the post office door.

"Back probably shortly. Could be one hour or maybe a bit longer. Stuff happens suddenly, eh?"

Cameron thought the notice had been meticulously penned for someone in a hurry, and a number of pinholes on each side suggested previous emergency uses.

"There she is." Rachel pointed down to the wharf, where *HMCS Carrier,* the water taxi that handled the mail collection and delivery, was sitting in the bay, playing Frank Mills's "Music Box Dancer" across the water, like a buoyant ice cream van.

The tall, bearded skipper, Alfie Cassidy, was standing aside to allow entry to the familiar Rubenesque form of Sarah Flynn. He closed the door.

Soon the vessel started into a rocking motion.

"She's collecting the mail," Rachel explained.

"Of course she is," Cameron agreed.

Sarah disembarked and walked, dewy-eyed and smiling, up the wharf, Canada Post satchel swinging at her side.

Cameron said, "Sarah, I'd like to ask you . . ."

"Think carefully about that job you've been offered in Toronto, Cameron. Spinner's Inlet is a pretty special place to work."

ER

"First, we separate the needy from the nosy and the malingering," Dr. Daisy Chen said, waving a dainty hand around her newly opened emergency ward. This was the freshly cleaned annex to the recently departed Dr. Timothy's office, the opening of which on this first day had attracted a sudden flurry of Inlet citizens, a number of whom fit Daisy's last two designated groups.

Nurse Patsy McFee grinned and examined the list of those who had appeared at the triage station—her desk—and announced their complaints.

Dr. Daisy had interviewed RN Patsy on Skype a month earlier, after Patsy had applied for the part-time position

Daisy had advertised. Patsy was moving to the Inlet with her husband, Duncan, who had bought an interest in a shake mill at the north end of the island.

Daisy had checked on Patsy's record of several years of work at Langley Memorial Hospital's Emergency Room and at two GP's offices, and texted her, "When can you start?" She was in the Inlet two days after that.

Patsy examined Finbar O'Toole as he approached her desk on crutches. The crutches were the folding type that can be packed away when not needed, which Patsy—having watched from the window as Finbar nimbly stepped from his pickup truck and deftly assembled them—thought was about now.

She checked Finbar's medical card. "What's the problem, Mr. O'Toole?"

"Legs," Finbar said. "Need a doctor's certificate to say I'm not fit to work, to go on disability."

"And the company you work for?"

"Er . . ."

"Your employer, the one who hired you?"

"Er . . ."

"They would have registered with WorkSafeBC and been paying premiums to cover injuries on the job so that you can claim benefits."

"Well . . . kinda self-employed . . ."

"Ah, so *you* would have been paying the premiums?"

"Er . . ."

"I'll have to make a couple calls. Take a seat over there." She indicated a line of metal chairs.

"Well . . ."

"A seat, Mr. O'Toole. Over there."

"*Finbar*, please," Finbar said, as ingratiating as all get out.

"Finbar it is. Seat anyway. Over there."

Finbar crutch-hopped to a chair, his eyes on the exit door.

The Clements kids were next, Alun holding Marathon, their SPCA rescue pup, in his arms, and Jillian sobbing.

"Paw," Alan said, and pointed to the pup's foot, which was bleeding from an embedded cedar splinter.

"Vet?" Patsy asked.

"Victoria," Jillian gulped. "Note said if emergency, see Dr. Daisy."

"Or Androcles?" the nurse suggested.

"Hah! Aesop!" Alun laughed.

Patsy smiled. "I'll get a little treat for him while we wait."

"No!" Alun said. "He's not allowed to eat between meals. Weight an' that."

His sister groaned and fondled the pup's ears.

Patsy bristled. "Bloody hell." Patsy knew about diets, everything from Dr. Atkins to Paleolithic—and had tossed all of them. "Half a damn Arrowroot biscuit!" she growled, and gave it to the willing, drooling, and seemingly now smiling Marathon.

Dr. Daisy appeared. "Little bit of freezing first," she said, and waved a hypodermic. "Have a seat for a while." Jillian crunched her eyes closed while Daisy administered the freezing. Alun bore the moment stoically, as did Marathon.

Dr. Daisy looked out the window at the sound of horse hoofs on the gravel road.

"Hell, I hope not," she groaned, then breathed out relief when Annabelle Bell-Atkinson trotted by on her Arab mare, Salome, riding sidesaddle. "She looks like she's in that series *Victoria*," Daisy said. "Let's hope she doesn't fall off anywhere near here." She gazed around the room. "Have you seen Penny?" she asked Patsy.

"Penny . . . ?"

"Littlebear. She missed this morning's prenatal class."

"No," Patsy said. "I'll phone the garden centre."

Penny was late teens, or maybe mid-teens. She had not been specific when she arrived in the Inlet a few months before from "up north," alone and pregnant—she wasn't sure quite since when—and did not mention the father. She had found a job at Widden's Garden Centre, and they allowed her to rent a room. She had been found to be industrious, conscientious, and reliable.

"She's done everything right until now," Daisy noted. "That girl could pop any second."

An audience had gathered; the nosy lot.

Rachel Spinner sat doing her own assessment of the lame and lazy as more wounded arrived. Young Sam Spinner had squashed flat a forefinger with a poorly aimed stone axe on a walling job. Legitimate. Randolph Champion said he was looking for some painkillers for a friend (unidentified). Rachel laughed out loud and Patsy pointed to the door. Geek Henry or Harvey shuffled furtively in, approached Patsy, and whispered in her ear. She tried not to smile, and told him to take a seat until Dr.

Daisy could see him. He grinned sheepishly at everyone and said, "Nothing serious."

There was a sudden fuss at the door, which slammed open, and Wilfred Widden called out, "Gangway, move aside." He propelled forward a two-wheeled garden-centre cart, normally used for moving plants and bags of soil, now holding a reclining and quietly moaning Penny Littlebear, who had decided that the need to complete a list of chores took precedence over imminent delivery.

Dr. Daisy waved Wilfred into the inner office, gave Penny a quick look-over, and said, "Glad you could make it."

Nurse Patsy announced to the gathered, "If you're just here to watch, go away. We have an emergency."

Twenty minutes later Daisy Littlebear, six pounds four ounces, was welcomed into the population of Spinner's Inlet. The stubbornly remaining audience was advised, and applauded heartily.

A moment later Finbar O'Toole apparently received a call on his cellphone. He took it from his pocket, said "Yeah?" and "Oh, dear." And to Patsy, "Sorry, bit of an emergency for me too," and turned to leave.

He had taken three steps when Patsy called, "Finbar?"

A hurried, "What?"

"Your crutches."

Neighbourly Treats

The Inlet was astir with rumours about the new people moving into the big house that sat atop and back from the long slope above the ferry terminal. The house had stood empty for two years before renovations started six months before. Local trades were politely turned down for the work; a gang of incomers and their tools and equipment arrived on the Monday ferry and left on Fridays, saying nothing.

But now there was movement, and an event, announced on *The Tidal Times*' front page. "A meet-and-greet from our new neighbours at their open house," with a two-hour window on Friday afternoon.

"That's exciting," Maggie Wilson said.

"I heard it's the Canucks' new goalie," one voice said. "Rolling in dough. Gonna commute to home games."

Another had heard it was a weekend getaway for U2, Bono having being smitten by the West Coast. "When he was hitchhiking that time in West Van and that Oilers' player, Gilbert Brule, picked him up and gave him a lift to Horseshoe Bay."

"All will be disclosed," Finbar O'Toole offered sagely.

The *Times* reminded its readers that it was a tradition in the Inlet to welcome new incomers with a small gift or, as an option, a personal skills performance.

Maggie Wilson (née Margarita Consuela Pereyra-Mendez) decided she would open proceedings on Friday, on the makeshift outdoor plywood stage, with a Spanish dance theme. (The house's occupants had apologized to the gathering for not inviting them inside because the place was still a work in progress.) Maggie had been practising the various styles—bachata, salsa, paso doble, and tango—alongside YouTube versions in front of the TV. She had abandoned the bachata, with its demanding side-to-side, hip-move requirements, when her left side locked and stayed that way for an hour.

She had also brought an Iberian-themed gift in the shape of a pair of castanets she claimed once belonged to one of General Franco's girlfriends. She had acquired them on her and Lennie's honeymoon. Maggie remembered the trip because at the Madrid airport, she had ordered a gin and tonic and the bartender, when he had finally quit pouring the gin, waiting for her to say "when," had no room left for the tonic. In the city she had noticed a souvenir stand with a handsome young fellow who waved her over. He brought the castanets out from an "especial" supply for the señorita—which Lennie gruffly corrected to "señora, now, pal"—and assured her of their provenance.

Maggie had giggled, and tried out her European. "*Merci*, mister."

To Lennie later, she smiled, "It was almost like he was expecting me."

"Saw you coming, anyway."

Now she clicked the castanets over her head and swooped into an Argentine tango, a dance that relies greatly on improvisation, which was a good thing for the unknowing spectators for whom Maggie's performance could have been anything, including some kind of mating dance. "Olé," she sang and did a thirty-second gig that left her panting.

Finbar O'Toole stepped up and predictably began his whining, dissonant version of "Danny Boy."

After two lines, "How can he be so bad?" Broadway-theatre-school-bound Connie Wilson mused.

"Practice," explained Samson Spinner, nearby. "Lots of practice."

Mark Clements, pilot, father of Alun and Jillian, and owner of the small and barely surviving float-plane charter outfit, waved a huge printed sign offering a one-time deal of twenty-five percent off his usual rates to Vancouver or Victoria for all new residents, or anyone else.

His sign was suddenly torn from his grip and flung into the bay about a hundred metres away by the

downdraft from a massive AgustaWestland AW101 helicopter, which roared in over the house and drifted down
to settle like a giant butterfly, or praying mantis, Mark
thought, on the front lawn of newly sodded turf.

Mark knew that anyone who could afford to fly in this
piece of advanced aviation technology, with a value of
$21-plus million and its three pilots, was not going to be
persuaded by his offer. Nor would he or she even deign
to step into his DHC-2 Beaver, even if he did clean out the
McDonald's wrappers and duty-free Jim Beam Red Stag
bottles dumped by his recent fares of three Americans
from Portland, who bitched about everything during the
ninety-minute trip to the fishing lodge west of Rivers Inlet,
and forgot to tip.

"Bastards," Mark said, all-inclusively.

His teacher wife, Julie, frowned at him and nodded
that the kids were close by. Jillian grinned and flashed her
dad a thumbs-up. Then she took off to the shoreline and
waded in to retrieve Mark's bargain-flight notice. Connie
Wilson went with her for company, and safety.

Hyacinth Jakes had arrived from the seniors residence. She waved at the faces now at the windows
of the big house and broke into "Abide with Me,"
ornamenting the hymn with a Hohner Special 20 harmon-
ica accompaniment.

"Almost like Dylan," noted Lennie Wilson, who was
standing well apart from Maggie as she rested after her
performance, fanning her face with anther souvenir from
their honeymoon trip. "A bit, anyway," he corrected, as
three of Hyacinth's chords veered sharply adrift.

The Reverend Amber Rawlings said, "Amen," as Hyacinth's final note faded, and then herself pitched in with "Amazing Grace."

The people inside the house had opened the windows and were applauding the performances: "Bravo!" and "Encore!" they called for the reverend, who was so inspired that she started to chant the Twenty-third Psalm before Rachel Spinner coughed loudly and indicated that there were others waiting to perform a welcoming act.

Or, in the case of Annabelle Bell-Atkinson, offer a gift.

With a flourish she swept the tea-towel cover off a tray of her appropriately named rock buns and laid it on the front step. The big double doors opened and a hand appeared and lifted the tray inside. Ten minutes later the tray was replaced, with a thank you note on it, and all of the buns intact except one with a bite out of it.

Erik Karlsson, great-great-nephew of the late Svensen and "Second Swede," as he had become known, hurried forward, took a stance with the five-string banjo he had recently purchased on Amazon along with an Earl Scruggs instruction book, and broke into the first bars of "Dueling Banjos." He paused, head cocked, and waited, apparently expecting the opposing duelling bit to start up from somewhere else, and when it didn't, played the opening riffs again . . . and again . . . and waiting . . .

At this point an exodus from the big house began, a line of people headed toward the ferry terminal. Two climbed into the giant helicopter—which was when things went awry. The expensive chopper had landed on a particularly soggy area on the sodded lawn, and had already begun to lean a tad to port. The addition of passengers finished the job; one wheel and its strut supports were suddenly below the surface.

A conference among the big bird's three pilots concluded that they were grounded for the immediate future.

"Shoot!" remarked someone in the remaining lineup. "I can't be late. Toronto connection!"

Connie Wilson pointed to the speaker. "That looks like Ryan Jackson! He's in that new series, *Coast Mysteries* or something. I'm sure that's him."

"He's in everything," Annabelle Bell-Atkinson grunted, apparently still affronted over her rock buns and not impressed by the renowned actor—if indeed that's who it was, though she had to admit it looked like him, as he turned a warm smile on Connie, who was helping Jillian hold up the rescued, though now dampish, sign.

The possible actor took a quick look. "Want to come for a ride?"

Connie grabbed Jillian's hand. "Let's go!"

"All aboard," said Mark Clements.

Gone and Back

"G'morning, Bernie," said Constable Ravina Sidhu, nodding at the items that were lined up on Bernie's lawn and driveway.

"Morning, Constable," Bernie Baranski replied. Then, "What?" at the smile that Ravina was failing to contain.

"Well, I've been getting complaints about someone living on his front lawn—hahahaha!"

"Gimme strength," Bernie said. "Know how many people have delivered that line this morning?"

Ravina sighed, sympathetic. "Well, it was a funny movie—*Everything Must Go*—and you do look a bit like Will Ferrell."

"I think I preferred *Kicking and Screaming*, the soccer thing with him and Robert Duvall," Bernie said. "And I'm sure I look more like Duvall. And apparently I can be as much of a dick."

Ravina nodded what seemed to be agreement as she watched Lennie Wilson examine the collection of stuff on the two gate-leg tables on Bernie Baranski's driveway and spilling over onto the lawn: hand tools, handbags, two laptops, an ancient LP record player, which anyone would consider a steal at fifteen dollars. Lennie offered ten dollars for the player and Bernie shrugged and said, "Take it."

"So, really? *Everything*, this time?" Ravina asked.

"This time" indicated her familiarity with the frequent disruptions in the relationship between Bernie and his wife, Barbara, disruptions that had led to previous announcements of separation, and driveway and lawn sales similar to this one, but never so comprehensive. Up to now there had been resolutions, usually involving tears and mutual self-recriminations. But this one seemed to have "the end" writ large on it for the couple who had endeared themselves to the Inlet population since they had set up house in an old cabin on the west side of the Inlet about four years before. Bernie dabbled in "financials" on the internet. Barbara painted abstracts ("Abstract 1," "Abstract 2," and so on)—which happened to be participants in the present conflict.

Since their arrival they had been the first to volunteer at community events, the last to leave the Summer Fiesta after cleaning up. They were the crossing guards at the elementary school when asked, and they organized and officiated at the seniors weekly bingo. It could be said that no one wanted to see them leave.

"Everything," Bernie said, nodding confirmation at the sign, which was attracting more interest by the minute, with people tut-tutting—"a shame" and other insincerities—but grabbing at the goods and checking the suggested prices.

Cameron Girard walked around and listened and made notes of the proceedings, which drew the attention of Annabelle Bell-Atkinson, whose name had not appeared in the local paper's pages for several weeks. "The media. Vultures. Picking people's bones." She then hovered over a set of two abacuses that seemed to be made of jade, asking price fourteen dollars. She looked around and pushed them to the back of the table, out of sight behind two ageing copies of the *Oxford English Dictionary*.

"Seven bucks," Randolph Champion said, holding up an almost-new Ryobi leaf blower with a label of forty-five dollars.

The Reverend Amber Rawlings, observing the action and apparently with nothing better to do and feeling the moment, murmured, "Jesus entered the temple courts and drove out all who were buying and selling there. He overturned the tables of the money changers and the benches of those selling doves," with a nod to an empty and rusting bird cage. "Matthew 21:12."

"Doves?" Bernie queried.

"What did Barbara say about this?" a just-arrived Anwen Brannigan enquired, while Randolph upped his offer by a buck, and a distracted Bernie shocked him by accepting. Anwen had become particularly close to Barbara and had suggested that Barbara start giving art classes for seniors such as herself and indeed had offered to pose "any way you like."

In fact it was Barbara's art that had sparked the present squabble and split. Bernie had in a moment of pique repeated the words of a fellow who sold occasional freelance pieces to the Victoria *Times Colonist* under the byline "Traveller" and who specialized in finding "remote and unrecognized artists." The critic had suggested, unkindly, that Barbara would for some time continue unrecognized unless someone like himself ("an acknowledged expert") developed an improbable fondness for her works, which he described as "resembling Rorschach ink blots, but without the latter's essential subtlety and charm."

When the review was published, Bernie had risen in fury and organized a petition to ban the capital city newspaper from the Inlet and "Traveller" from the BC Ferries system. Willie Whittle, who embodied the ferries in the Inlet, in a demonstration of the "us-against-them" spirit typical of the community, said that while nothing official could be done, people could be assured that the workers' grapevine would see that any future ferry ride that insulting sonofabitch took would not be a happy one. It was believed that the man had taken to wearing disguises to get around.

"She's gone," Bernie told Anwen. "Long gone."

"How long?"

Bernie turned to deal with the Clements kids, who were holding tight to an ancient Smith-Corona portable typewriter and a box of four hard-to-find new ribbons. Alun had read of a rising interest in old typewriters and had persuaded Jillian that they could start a used-goods business if they could knock Bernie down to fifteen dollars from his asking price of forty.

"Get him while he's distracted," Alun said. "I've read that that works in bargaining."

"Morning ferry," Bernie replied to Anwen.

"He's right, I seen her get aboard," said Willie Whittle, who had shut down the ferry ticket office ("back in ten or so") to take a look at Bernie's clear-out sale and had his eyes on a newish-looking electric hedge clipper at a giveaway seven-fifty.

"Take it," Bernie said to the kids, and indifferently accepted a ten and a five from Jillian.

"Going where?" Anwen asked. "I mean after Tsawwassen."

Bernie shrugged. "It's a very big world out there. She has a sister in Burnaby and a cousin way out in Mission. So who knows?"

Sheila Martin had wandered up as the kids were doing their deal. "Take that right home, and keep it there. No craigslist or eBay. Do we understand?" In the tone that grandmas use that isn't really a question. A nearby Rachel Spinner nodded her approval of Sheila's order, and she and Sheila continued on their way to catch the *Gulf Queen* to Tsawwassen. Cameron Girard exchanged a nod and a smile with her as she passed.

Anwen Brannigan said, "So you're getting rid of everything of hers."

"Everything that reminds me of her," Bernie said.

"Like the grass trimmer?" Almost new but offered at twenty dollars and being fondled by Jackson Spinner, who had let the grass around the B & B get long enough to conceal dogs, cats, and small children.

"We had a deal that she did the edges and I mowed the lawn. It can go."

"So it's worse than last time, then," Anwen said.

Last time was a spat after Bernie had overstayed a visit to the Cedars pub and arrived in the early hours bellowing out the Polish national anthem. "Poland is not yet lost," he yodelled. The neighbours turned on their lights, Hyacinth Jakes led a panicked exodus from the seniors complex, and Constable Ravina turned up and issued a stern warning against disturbing the peace, while keeping a straight face.

This time Bernie had moved Barbara's easel to make room in her studio for a new table saw. He knocked over the easel, punched a hole in the canvas that had been on it, picked up the untitled painting, held it at arm's length, and laughed, just as Barbara entered the room.

When Barbara chastised him, Bernie muttered, "Ink blots." And that was it.

Bernie sighed. "Yes, worse."

He turned and accepted the ten dollars offered by Jackson, who had the grace to look embarrassed as he took off with the trimmer.

Anwen shrugged and hurried away to catch up

with Sheila Martin and Rachel Spinner on their way to the ferry.

Bernie's tables were soon bare.

The following evening, after the *Gulf Queen*'s last arrival, there was a meeting at Rachel Spinner's house, and then they began the rounds.

Lennie Wilson came to his door. He listened and frowned, then, "But it was twenty bucks."

Rachel cocked an eyebrow at Cameron Girard. The reporter checked his notebook. "Ten dollars. At 1:26 PM." And "Thank you," holding out his hand with the ten-spot. Lennie pouted, then went and retrieved the player.

Cameron confirmed prices at each stop—or corrected for those with a short memory of events such as Randolph Champion who insisted he had forked over eighteen dollars for Bernie's new leaf blower and complained, "A deal should be a deal between people with principles." Rachel handed him his eight dollars and told him to get the tool and stop whining.

Willie Whittle handed over the hedge clipper, saying he would be glad to get his conscience clear.

Alun Clements wanted to negotiate, but his sister said there would be other opportunities, especially if some other couples she could mention might decide to untie the knot and clear out, and they should consider it part of the learning curve of starting a business in today's world of cut and thrust and dog eat dog. She had been talking with her dad, who was struggling with his float-plane charter venture. She handed over the typewriter and accepted fifteen dollars.

Rachel piled all the items into her pickup, said, "Right, then," to the other three who had joined her in "Exercise Fix-it," and they left, accompanied by Barbara, whom they had tracked the previous day to her cousin up the Fraser Valley and persuaded to return with them on the *Gulf Queen*.

Bernie Baranski listened closely as Barbara explained the conditions of her return—no table saw in her studio, not one negative comment about her art, no singing of the Polish national anthem outdoors—and pointed out those he had to thank for it.

Bernie took a vinyl disk out of its paper cover, touched it to his lips, and reverently placed it on the record player.

Barbara explained when the music started that it was a Polish wedding anniversary song that said in part, "You are my heart's reflection, and no one could ever take your place. Not one out of 7.5 billion."

"So romantic," she said. "Time for an abstract, I think."

Pressing the Matter

The British Columbia Press Council announced it would hold its next hearing in Spinner's Inlet. The council had been idle for some years but recently had decided to resurrect itself following a number of complaints concerning *The Tidal Times* and its publisher/editor/owner Silas Cotswold.

The hearing began in the community hall, which was packed.

Council chair Ms. Alice Buchanan, a prominent businessperson in Vancouver, said, "Let us establish that the council's code of practice states that a newspaper's first duty is to provide the public with accurate information, and that newspapers should correct inaccuracies promptly."

Heads turned toward Silas, who had parked himself on a seat in the front row. He smiled.

"We are confident that reasonable people generally are able to reach a resolution." She added that given that Silas Cotswold was himself a former professional member of the press council, representing the print journalism element, she expected that he would lend a particular level of professionalism to the event.

She announced the first complainant and read the details. "Annabelle Bell-Atkinson"—Annabelle stood and waved to a flurry of applause, and a few jeers, which brought a frown and a no-no wagged finger from the chair—"alleges that *The Tidal Times* in an editorial slandered her and her two nephews by describing the nephews as 'hazards to society' and herself as 'a newly minted Lady Macbeth.'" She turned to Silas. "Mr. Cotswold?"

Silas stood and stretched tall. He could be imposing when he wore his best Harris tweeds complete with Francis waistcoat and sturdy, laced Oxford brogues, which raised him a couple of centimetres, and halfglasses of the type that you look over the top of and appear intelligent.

He shook his head, apparently at such foolishness. "When the woman does not know the difference between slander and libel, how can we take her seriously? If it's in print, it's libel."

Annabelle seethed. The geeks Henry and Harvey pointed what seemed to be threatening fingers at Silas and the stage area in general, which caused the chair to take two steps back from the mic.

The geeks for years had memberships in Mensa, were rightly considered by their aunt to be geniuses, but were bereft of the simplest of social skills and, "They excite very easily," Annabelle explained.

Ms. Buchanan recovered and asked Silas, "So *was* it in print and *did* you therefore libel them?"

Silas sighed. "If it was, there was a good reason for it, and we all know what that is."

All waited.

Finally, "What?" from the chair.

"The basis of all good journalism, and known as the best defence against such scurrilous claims: the truth."

"He also called me a buffoon!" Annabelle roared.

"I rest my case," Silas said, and returned to his chair.

Buchanan turned and conferred in whispers with one of her two press council colleagues.

"The case will be considered," she said, "and the council will announce a ruling in due course."

She introduced a new issue. "Now, a further complaint, from," she checked her notes, "actually it is anonymous, but we are inclined to consider it, given the serious nature of the allegation. The person says that while they were never specifically named in a particular column by the editor, the whole community knew that they were being targeted when the said column criticized 'a number of layabouts who need not be identified and who give the community a bad reputation.' It said, 'One of them pretends to be the people's saviour and boasts of a history of civil disobedience and violence against the establishment, from whom he gladly accepts pogey and subsidized ferry fares.'"

Randolph Champion jumped to his feet. "Objection! I have never been given a break on the ferries! I didn't even know that was available."

Ms. Buchanan smiled. "There appears to be a need for clarification on the matter of fee structure by the BC Ferries Corporation."

"Guilty," said Silas. "And withdrawn."

"Now," the chair said, ominously, "a question of phone hacking by a member of *The Tidal Times* staff. The complaint is vague, the staff member is not named, and by normal standards we would pass on it, but given the history of such things in the UK, where one newspaper, the *News of the World*, was shut down because of it . . ."

Cameron Girard, the only member of the staff, other than Anwen Brannigan who dusted and cleaned up, looked up, startled. Moi? His lips formed.

Silas stepped in. "What exactly was gleaned from this supposed hacking? Allegedly."

Ms. Buchanan studied her notes. "Apparently, a conversation between your mayor, Sheila Martin, and a company in Victoria from which she had purchased an office desk to be paid for COD, and that she was threatening to refuse to accept until a new price could be agreed on, because the desk had a chip out of one corner, for which she was blaming the truck driver . . ."

Silas laughed.

The chair continued. "This conversation, a private

conversation, was printed verbatim in *The Tidal Times*, an act, the mayor claims, that brought into ridicule her office and the position of mayor."

At that point a cellphone rang out loudly—The Beatles' "Yesterday"—and kept ringing. All eyes went to the mayor, who was madly pressing the buttons on her phone, from which the tone was rising.

As the sound persisted, and Sheila failed to quell it, the Clements twins raced up to their grandma and between them, shut the sound off. "No, *this* one. We've told you, over and over," Jillian said, while Alun stood back, shook his head, and muttered, "What will it take?"

Silas laughed, and stood. "I was the so-called 'hacker,' but I didn't have to hack anything, even if I'd known how."

Henry or Harvey leaped to his feet. "I can teach you! It's dead easy!" he yelled. And added, "You great dummy." He was removed at the chair's request.

Silas continued. "She told me to wait outside her office—she used to be a teacher. I was waiting to interview her on some civic matters, but I accidentally overheard the conversation that she had made public by having put her phone on speaker."

Jillian said, "Grandma!" Her brother laughed out loud.

"He was eavesdropping!" Sheila shouted.

"A legitimate exercise for any reporter," Silas countered. "And anyway, you could have heard her in Nanaimo."

At this stage Sheila's phone rang again, and her daughter's voice boomed, "Mom. Are the kids with you?"

Snickers from the audience.

Ms. Buchanan looked at Sheila and shrugged. Then

checked the clock. "I'm afraid we're running short, time for just one more complaint, and this one from a well-known politician, your local MLA, Mr. Jethro Wallace. This concerns a conversation that apparently had privacy guaranteed but was reported in full and caused the aggrieved Mr. Wallace 'great embarrassment and damage to my reputation.'"

"There's an oxymoron," from the back row.

The case apparently involved a phone call from Jethro to Silas. The MLA was responding to Silas's questions about something he had heard about a clerk of the legislature questioning Jethro over expense claims he had submitted. These concerned business lunches with a contractor who was seeking government support for a condominium development in another part of Wallace's riding.

In answer to Silas, asking if the clerk had a case in claiming that it was the developer who had paid for all the lunches, Jethro had said, "Anyone can make a mistake."

Ms. Buchanan said, "Mr. Wallace claims, 'I told Cotswold that the conversation was off the record and he broke a sacred confidence in repeating it.'"

Silas stood. "An example of a common misunderstanding of the term 'off the record.' Both parties must agree to that being the case beforehand—that it *will be* off the record, not *was*, after the fact. If I listen and record what you say, then after you have done the damage you say, 'What I told you of course was off the record,' you're too late. And I did include at the end of the piece that he had said it was all off the record."

From the back of the hall, a late-arrived Jethro. "To make me look stupid."

Silas said, "I rest that case, too."

The press council members politely declined an invitation from Silas for "a spot of tea," and seemed to be in a hurry as they headed for the ferry.

Find the Artist

The mysterious artwork appeared overnight. No one had a clue as to the artist, though some opinions were offered.

Some of the works were simple stick figures, others fully formed. Some seemingly in charcoal, others in glowing spray paint, heavy brush strokes, light pencil lines, oil, rough acrylic . . . name a medium.

Drawings. Everywhere.

The one on the cedar-siding wall of Gilbert's Groceries was an accurate depiction of Gilbert Chen, complete with his shapeless green coverall. One might be forgiven for thinking it comprised his only wardrobe, given that anyone making a social call to Gilbert's house would find him answering the door wearing the same garment.

The post office wall featured a portrait of lawyer Ezekial Watson, handing out his business card, with one eye closed in a pronounced wink. On the back of the school gym was a flattering and shapely image of former teacher Mayor Sheila herself, reminiscent of when she would step in and take a phys-ed class and change into brief shorts for the occasion. It showed her shooting a basket. The image was svelte, or at least considerably less full than today's reality, and Sheila was quietly pleased with the effect.

MLA Jethro Wallace appeared on the ferry dock, in one of those clever illusion jobs that made him appear about to step off the edge. *The Tidal Times* picked up that one and ran a photo of the image on the front page.

The next day the illusion art on the dock had been changed: An upside-down bowler hat appeared, with a few coins and bills in and alongside it. The cash also was illusory, as Willard Starling from the seniors residence discovered when he attempted to pick it up. He almost joined Jethro, who in this version was now nose-down in the bay. The Bell-Atkinson geeks found this one especially amusing, pointing at Willard and howling at his wobbling near miss. Willard waved his cane at them and they strutted off, laughing. One pointed to the Jethro-in-the-water piece and they howled again and swapped high-fives.

The subject of the images dominated the letters page of *The Tidal Times:* A disgrace, some said. No better than the common graffiti vandals known as "taggers." It's time the guilty were apprehended.

"Nonsense," said another. "Consider what Banksy has done for the world of street art. We could be witnessing a genius among us. Maybe he's even visiting us on the quiet, or at least has sent a representative."

This, predictably, spurred Silas Cotswold to offer a challenge in *The Tidal Times*: "Find the artist. Identify this mystery artist and win a trip to the Pacific National Exhibition, courtesy of your local newspaper." (The tickets would be freebies provided to news outlets by the annual fair. Silas did not mention that winners would have to pay their ferry fares and any other expenses to get to the East Van celebration.)

The images usually appeared overnight.

Randolph Champion became a suspect when it was seen that he was refreshing some of his standard protest signs (the words "FOR" at the top, and "AGAINST" below, with a blank space awaiting fulfilment between and below them) with a hand-lettered Brush Script font. When Cameron Girard subtly questioned him, Randolph indelicately advised Cameron that he was using Microsoft Word to download any font he preferred and was simply tracing over the lettering by hand. "As even you could do if you tried," he said.

Others joined in the investigation. Annabelle Bell-Atkinson reported that she had seen an item on Facebook describing how Kiwi exchange teacher Jack Steele, as a young student, had won a national portrait–painting competition with a likeness of then-New Zealand Governor General Sir Michael Hardie Boys.

Jack responded. "I was very young and foolish, and the *New Zealand Herald* disclosed that I had used a paint-by-numbers kit. The GG himself forgave me and commended me for my initiative." He added, "I have not touched a paintbrush since."

Finbar O'Toole, on one of his regular visits to Dr. Daisy Chen's office, noticed that nurse Patsy McFee's desk was littered with prescription pads filled with stick drawings.

"Aha!" he said.

Patsy pointed to a partly finished gallows on one of the pads. "Dr. Daisy and I are playing Hangman, you clown," Patsy said. "And she's worse at spelling than I am. Now, consider yourself having been checked and found perfectly well, and bugger off."

Jackson Spinner told a group at the Cedars pub, "I think I have him!"

He described a young man who had checked in to his and Evelyn's B & B two days before the images appeared. "Checked in as Pietro something. Fancy hairdo, earrings in each side, tattoos from the knees up—he has one of those flat briefcase things that could hold all manner of artist stuff. When I asked him what he intended to paint, he said, 'Paint? Me?' Now if that doesn't sound like a Banksy-type . . ."

The door opened and a young man with hair down to his shoulders, earrings in each side, and tattoos all over, walked in and said, "Good evening."

"Petey!" Cedars' owner Matthew Blacklock, just returned from a week in Victoria, had the young fellow in a bear hug. "You came early!"

Matthew explained to the crowd. "My nephew. My sister's kid. Susie, the one married to the Italian off Commercial Drive. Calls himself 'Pietro'—actually it's 'Peter.' Creative type. Brought all his own gear."

He caught the glances, and laughed. "No, no. Not *him*. Petey is taking over the barbershop."

The Inlet had been without a barber since Jacques "The Clipper" Bouche had hung up his scissors and retired to Tofino for the surfing.

"Hot shaves a specialty," Peter announced with a flourish, noting the several stubbly faces in attendance.

Meanwhile, the images had begun fading, as had the enthusiasm for finding the artist.

"No winner, then, Silas," Samson Spinner said.

"A mystery still," Cotswold said. "Must be brains behind it, as well as talent."

No more images appeared, and the PNE closed its doors for another year.

Constable Ravina Sidhu finished her one after-shift glass of the Cedars' house red and left for home. She figured it must have been the slight buzz from the wine when she heard the geeks arguing as she passed the Bell-Atkinson home, but it sounded as if Henry, or Harvey, said, "No, leave that sonofabitch Wallace in the water."

At the Ready

"Community Emergency Plan—Public Meeting." The announcement was across the bottom of the first page of *The Tidal Times*. "Bring your suggestions on Friday night to the community hall."

The meeting was the idea of Annabelle Bell-Atkinson, lately returned from a vacation to Florida where an expected tropical storm had turned into an unexpected hurricane, sending thousands running for cover and Annabelle heading home.

Beside Annabelle on the stage was wildly unpopular MLA Jethro Wallace, who announced that due to his particular influence ("Order, please. Order!"), he had managed to arrange for the expert appearance of the second in command to the assistant of the associate deputy co-ordinator of provincial emergency services, whom he expected any moment now. "He has a Ph.D. in survival techniques."

Annabelle recalled her own experience down south. "It was a lesson in unpreparedness for a hurricane. We should never let it happen here."

"We don't get hurricanes," Evelyn Spinner said.

"Typhoon Freda, October 1962," corrected Henry or Harvey. "Same thing. Blew Stanley Park to bits."

"That's my cousin's name, Freda!" declared nurse Patsy McFee. "Coincidence, eh?"

"And if we did," Evelyn persisted, "E & J's B & B has more than enough rooms ready to accommodate the needy." She winked at Jackson sitting nearby. He gave her both thumbs up.

"Earthquake, then," Annabelle countered, becoming a bit testy. "The Big One. Lights out. No power. No water. What then?"

"The shelter!" The geeks chimed in as one.

"Oh, Christ, spare us," Samson Spinner said, as groans echoed all about.

The geeks' survival shelter had been under construction for the better part of a decade. The initial hole had been dug with a Caterpillar excavator that the geeks had hot-wired and borrowed one midnight from the site where the high school now stood. They had returned it before breakfast and denied any knowledge of the tractor-tread marks leading from their project to that site.

Most of the population of Spinner's Inlet had endured a tour of the shelter at one time or another.

When the geeks had demonstrated that once you were inside, there was no way out unless you knew the code to punch in to the keypad that controlled the massive, steel-reinforced door, former community physician Dr. Timothy, a confirmed claustrophobic, had suffered a panic attack while ensuring that he was in between the geeks and the still-open door, and later needed a double Scotch to get over it.

"There's only room for four in there," Samson said. "Two bunk beds."

"And only beans to eat," added young Alun Clements.

He and Jillian had counted the endless rows of Campbell's pork and beans on the shelves the geeks had built. The geeks had seen a case-lot sale advertised in a flyer from Nanaimo and had snagged the lot.

"Can you imagine that place closed up and whoever is in there eating all those beans?" Jillian said, and Alun broke into, "Beans, beans, the musical fruit, the more you eat the more you toot . . ."

"Let's move on," Annabelle said. "We could use this very hall, should it remain standing. We could gather here, do a head count, and see who has brought what to help us all through."

She checked the hall clock and her wristwatch. "Our guest, the second in command to the assistant of the . . . thingamajiggy . . . seems to be running a bit late. But as I was saying, we will need . . ."

"Bottled water, lots of bottled water," Gilbert Chen

offered. "It's on special this week," he added. "At Gilbert's Groceries."

"We'd be looking for *donations*," Annabelle breathed.

"How about toilet paper?" Jillian said. "I was just in the john here and there's no more left after this roll gets done. Which it almost is. And it's getting old. When I tore the last three sheets off . . ."

Her mother gave her the "Enough" signal.

Randolph Champion called out, "I could provide signs for the highway with arrows saying, 'A new life this way,' and, 'Give me your poor, your tired, your huddled masses . . .'"

"We're not expecting refugees," Annabelle said. Then, "Well, not any *more* refugees," with a nod to the Hanif family sitting in the front row. Ali Hanif gave Annabelle two thumbs up. Ali's youngest child, his son, Fabian, offered a different digit signal, product of a growing affiliation with some of his peers at the elementary school. This brought a fierce glare from Annabelle and howls of laughter from the geeks, who responded to Fabian's gesture with vigorous flourishes of their own.

Ali's wife, Aila, having come to understand plenty of the baser elements of her new society (she had Netflix and had accidentally tuned in to an occasional rapper), missed her son's signal, and interpreted the reciprocal responses as Annabelle and the geeks insulting her family. She rose in a snit and left, followed by a puzzled Ali, a grinning Fabian, and the Hanifs' two daughters, Nadia and Balour, the latter blowing the geeks a loud raspberry because she felt someone should do something to defend the family's honour, and she too was becoming familiar with local habits.

"Must have been something you said," Samson Spinner advised Annabelle, who demanded the meeting get back to its purpose.

"Prayer sheets," the Reverend Amber Rawlings called out. "We will need them if we are going to praise the Lord and hope for His assistance."

"Or Hers," Jillian murmured.

"I'm an atheist." From the back, Erik Karlsson, great-great-nephew of the still-much-lamented Svensen.

"Bless you anyway," Reverend Amber smiled. "There will always be room for you around our campfires, which we will surely be needing when . . . er, They send the Big One. We will pray and sing . . ."

Kiwi exchange teacher Jack Steele strummed an air guitar and broke into, "Kumbaya, my Lord . . ."

"Hymns."

Most of the audience joined Jack and heartily sang the four verses down to and through "Someone's praying, Lord . . ." etc.

By now the meeting had fallen apart and Annabelle announced above the noise that as it appeared that no one seemed prepared take her seriously, they might as well all go home.

Cameron Girard's report in *The Tidal Times* next day said the meeting had ended on a high note but that MLA Wallace's acclaimed Ph.D. in survival had failed to show.

This was explained to Cameron later that day with a

phone call from a colleague at the Victoria *Times Colonist* newspaper. "The guy was at a seminar in the morning. It was titled 'Advice to provincial government staff on dealing on-site with our outlying communities, such as Spinner's Inlet, and their inhabitants.' He apparently went straight home from that and phoned in sick for the rest of the day."

New York

"Student visa." The young man in the uniform of a US Customs and Border Protection agent sighed and repeated the words, slowly. "Stu-dent vi-sa."

Charlie Wilson looked at his daughter, Connie. *Well?* They had half an hour before their flight left Toronto for LaGuardia in New York.

Connie shook her head. She shuffled again through the pile of papers in her hands. No visa there.

"If you don't have a stamped student visa, you cannot be allowed into the United States as a student, can you? Make sense? We can't have just anybody and everybody entering the country."

Charlie thought of the thousands of "irregulars" who had walked across the border from the US into Canada's welcoming arms in the recent past. Not a visa among them.

They had shown the paperwork from the American Musical and Dramatic Academy (AMDA) that showed that Connie had been awarded a substantial but not full scholarship based on the audition she had given in Vancouver. A portion to be paid, plus travel.

Connie pointed to her folder again. "That's all I got."

The young man ("Valadez" on his chest-mounted nameplate) sighed. "I'll talk to someone," he left.

Twenty-five minutes to go.

Charlie wondered for a second if declaring themselves refugees might work. He had managed to acquire the funds that would get his daughter to New York and decided that she should not make the first trip alone but needed a street-smart companion. (He put aside the memory of becoming lost at Pike Place Market on his first trip to Seattle and needing help to locate the Space Needle on his second.) The community of Spinner's Inlet had been generous once it was understood the money was for Connie, and not Charlie.

The Inlet Players had donated all the takings from a three-night run of *Playboy of the Western World*. Constable Ravina Sidhu had hinted to Cedars pub owner Matthew Blacklock that to donate one night's takings would be a small thing compared with a surprise visit from a BC Liquor and Cannabis Regulation Branch inspector who might be interested in what was really meant by "last orders." And Gilbert Chen had stuck small flags onto certain items in the store bearing the words, "Yea, Connie!" and a matching cash box on the counter.

Valadez returned with a large woman in agent uniform, who said, "Canadians, eh? *Eh?*" and chuckled at her wit. She grilled them about their past. Charlie waited nervously for the cannabis question, but the woman passed on it.

Twenty minutes.

The woman started chatting about the differences between their two countries, especially the rules for border crossing, and Charlie looked at the clock.

Fifteen minutes.

Finally she stamped a temporary visa and gave them an address in New York where they *must* appear. "If you make your plane right now, that is," she said.

They did, with no time left.

Charlie thought there might be time for a quick beer when they landed at LaGuardia. It was after five o'clock and he would welcome that familiar feeling of well-being always fashioned by the first few sips of suds. Connie grabbed her bag and pointed to the taxi rank.

The cabbie, a native of Haiti, as he would tell them, advised them to lock their doors as he did his own. He chatted as they passed through neighbourhoods from Robert De Niro scripts, explaining, while narrowly avoiding challenges to his driving at several inter-sections, that he was a retired army sergeant, and he engaged them with his philosophy that it was unwise for other drivers to mess with a New York cabbie. And any that did with him, he would kill, he said. Charlie laughed. The driver didn't.

The driver said that normally, he would not have the cab's dividing window open, but "You seem like different kinda folks."

Connie caught Charlie's glance: *we're* different?

They paused at an intersection and three youths wearing camo-patterned do-rags stepped toward the cab and peered inside. The driver lowered his window and growled something; the trio retreated.

How on earth, Charlie thought, was Connie going to survive in this place?

As they left the cab—and a hefty tip that Charlie considered the judicious thing to do—a banjo busker across the street from the hotel where they would spend their first night was singing "The Streets of New York," a song Charlie knew well as one of the many Celtic laments Finbar O'Toole droned at the Cedars' open mic nights.

> *"And remember all is not*
> *What it seems to be,*
> *For there's fellas would cut ye*
> *For the coat on yer back,*
> *Or the watch that ye got*
> *From yer mother . . ."*

Charlie shuddered.

The address the woman agent had given them was at Federal Plaza in downtown Manhattan, where they headed at noon the next day after Connie had registered at AMDA and where it seemed that hundreds of people moved at a snail's pace in a line behind rows of control barriers.

Charlie went straight to the building's front door and explained confidently to the ex-NFL lineman guarding the place with a large revolver on his belt that they simply needed a stamp on a student visa and that "We are Canadians, so . . ."

The big man pointed them to the back of the line. Connie groaned, and sneezed. She was developing a cold. It was a sunny day and she had worn a thin blouse, but they were in the shadows of inconceivably huge buildings and a chilling wind cut through their canyons. They waited in the outside lineup for ninety minutes before they were admitted through the door—and into the first of three long and winding inside lineups. Half an hour took them to a wicket where a young male clerk listened, unimpressed, as Charlie explained their situation.

"You should be on the tenth floor, Room 104," he said, and looked up and said, "Next," as their number light (521) became history.

"You mean we needn't have waited all this time . . ."

"Tenth floor, Room 104."

In Room 104 an immigration officer was advising a man. "I remember arresting you at JFK. If you are lying now, you are in *big* trouble."

Charlie believed him.

The officer turned to Charlie. "Where's your yellow referral slip?"

"No one gave us . . ."

"You have to have it."

Back to the main floor where a mood of desperation mounted in the lineups as the business day neared its end.

"Sorry," the man behind the desk said, "but we're closin'."

"But . . ."

"Come back tomorrow. Seven AM."

"To this desk?"

He shook his head. No. He nodded to the main door. To start all over.

"Oh, noooo," Connie groaned.

The man shrugged, sympathetic. "Canadians. I really don't know why we bother about visas."

But they do.

Charlie believed in the philosophy "Never say never." Elevator back to 104.

"No yellow slip," he told the officer, fervently. "They're shutting shop and we have to start the whole bloody thing over tomorrow."

The officer shrugged.

Connie sagged.

The officer shook his head. He sighed. "Wait," he said.

Charlie thought this was an improvement on the "Stay!" command earlier from one of the man's colleagues to a fellow on the ground floor. The fellow had stayed.

Ten minutes and the officer relented. He laid his precious stamp on the critical paper.

"And good luck at school," he smiled.

Charlie figured maybe just a beer somewhere before they moved on. Connie voted for move on, lots to do.

188

Connie's "shared accommodation" (shared with whom?) was in an ageing, red-brick, ten-storey apartment building where a notice said, "KEEP YOUR DOORS LOCKED AT ALL TIMES" and urged those students arriving by car to "LEAVE SOMEONE WITH YOUR VEHICLE WHILE PARKING TO REGISTER."

Good grief!

"Top floor, Dad."

The room at least was clean. Two cots with bedding stacked on them. Two built-in closets and two sets of table and chair. Common bathroom down the hall. The view from the window was straight out of *West Side Story*. Flat, black-top roofs. A screaming fire truck parted the traffic.

The door banged open. A girl examined them, said, "Y'all the Canadian, right?"

"Both of us," Charlie said.

"Ah'm Katie. From Texas. Y' roommate, Con."

Con?

Katie hugged Connie.

"Canadians, eh?" A large man at the door, carrying two travel bags. Texas hat, Texas belt buckle, Texas boots. A petite blonde woman entered behind him, chiding, "C'mon, move it, Chester." And, "Ah'm Callie Boone— really, lahk Daniel. Hello, honey." Callie hugged Connie. "Let's get this place put together, you two. Y'all gonna be great together. Ah know it."

She ushered Chester and Charlie aside, and within a minute the two men might not have been there as cots were agreed on and made up and other major decisions made.

Chester grinned at Charlie. "They'll be fahn, y'know," he said. He gestured toward the window and across and down to a flashing sign on what turned out to be Amsterdam Avenue. Red-and-green neon: McLeary's.

"Ahrish pub, Ah believe."

Callie turned to them. "One hour," she said. "Then you take us all to dinner. Shoo," she added. "We got woman stuff to do."

Charlie looked at Connie.

"Go, Dad," she said. She smiled. "And thank you."

Charlie nodded at his new friend Chester. "My round," he said.

Pets and Plants

It was decided that next year, the Spinner's Inlet Owners and Pets Day and the Harvest Festival would revert to being held as separate occasions.

The Reverend Amber Rawlings conceded that her suggestion of holding them in concert had turned out to be much better in theory than in practice. "I really thought that harmony might prevail," she said.

The Tidal Times had echoed her sentiment, saying that the day would "bring pets and friends together with cooks and gardeners in an amicable atmosphere and spirit of competition."

"Shouldn't that be '*animal*' atmosphere," young Alun

Clements had said. Jillian snorted. Alun was fairly close, as it happened.

Things began going sideways when Danny Sakiyama pointed Finbar O'Toole to the other side of the five-barred gate that led to the events field. "It's a bloody horse. We do pets," Danny said.

Danny was marshal and chief judge for all the annual goings-on. His word was law. As the community letter carrier for just about ever, and thus privy to a particular store of private material, he was known and respected—and a little feared—by all.

"It's a Shetland pony!" Finbar argued. "Look." He stood astride the somewhat plump Nelly, his feet touching the ground, nothing touching the animal. Or pet. "Watch," he said. He took a carrot stick from his pocket, held it about a foot below Nelly's left shoulder. The pony—brushed shiny and beribboned with Irish Republican green, white, and orange ribbons—folded at the knees, snaffled the carrot, and whinnied an apparent thank you.

"She's named for my granny in Rathdrum, County Wicklow," Finbar said. "Obviously a pet, 'cause who would name an actual horse after his granny?"

A dispute in the other half of the field grew louder, between the tables reserved separately for fruit and vegetables, next to the ones for baked goods, jams, and sauces.

"It's a fruit," stated Dr. Daisy's nurse, Patsy McFee. She plopped a plump Better Boy tomato on the judging table and pointed to the definition copied from the *Oxford English Dictionary* that she carried with her everywhere in case of such a dispute. "The glossy fleshy FRUIT . . ."

She shouted the last bit, causing heads to lift and people to drift toward what promised to be something of a barney.

"Fruit my foot. When did you last make a fruit soup?" Anwen Brannigan demanded.

They kept at it, while at the gate Finbar was pointing apparently in disbelief and mouthing, "What the f . . . what the f . . . ?"

"Correct, a female lion," Eddie Pape explained. "Sit, Fatima." He tugged on the retractable leash that attached him to the big cat. Fatima growled, stared speculatively at Nelly, but sat.

Finbar, who owned a copy of *Bartlett's Familiar Quotations*, decided to heed Falstaff's suggestion that "Caution is preferable to rash bravery." In other words, he chose discretion over valour, and conceded, "Okay, animal, not pet," and, "Gee-up" as he pointed Nelly homeward. "And that's a pet?" as Fatima settled down at Eddie's feet.

A sudden interjection was offered from the sideline. "Neither of them are pets. There are no such things as pets." A young woman wearing a large, round badge proclaiming her a member of People for the Ethical Treatment of Animals (PETA).

Then Jillian Clements said, "She means neither of them *is* a pet." She had become sensitive to subject-verb agreement since her grandma, Sheila Martin, in retired-teacher mode, got onto her about it.

"They are animal companions," the PETA member said.

Fatima opened wide her large, orangey-brown eyes.

Eddie said, "Easy, Fatima." The lioness growled.

Danny Sakiyama said, "Er, Eddie . . ." but nothing else.

Edward "Eddie" Pape had been given some leeway in the matter of keeping wildlife as pets. He was a native of Senegal and a member of that national soccer team, as well as of Tottenham Hotspurs of the English Premier League. His Spurs status had been somewhat compromised the previous season because of a tricky knee, which had seen the team place him on the available-for-loan list, whence the Vancouver Whitecaps, in their usual panic for an effective striker, had taken him for the season.

Eddie had explained in an interview with Cameron Girard that just before leaving Senegal, he had seen Fatima, one of the few remaining lions in his country, lying in a ditch badly injured from an encounter with a Toyota pickup. He had nursed her back to health and finessed her through officialdom on his way to Tottenham, and then to Vancouver. While it was officially illegal to keep such a beast as a "pet," with intercessions by the premier, who himself had been a fairly decent fullback, and who never missed a Whitecaps game, certain allowances had been made . . .

Eddie's wife, Bernadette, had taken a cruise of the islands while the negotiations were concluding, had stopped at Spinner's Inlet, and decided that a chunk of Eddie's transfer fee would be well spent on a cabin for rent for the year at the south end of the Inlet. Eddie scored a hat-trick on his first appearance for the 'Caps, against the Seattle Sounders, making him and Bernadette eligible for instant citizenship in the minds of all 'Caps fans.

With French being Senegal's official language, Bernadette had been grabbed by the Spinner's Inlet school board, which had been desperate for a teacher for the summer immersion session.

"I thought I might enter her in the exotic pets section," Eddie said. "If you have one."

"Of course we do," Danny said.

"Now, anyway," Jillian said.

"Still not a pet," said PETA, who had stepped back a bit.

"I'll tell her that," Eddie said, beaming a smile.

From across the field, at the green-plants table. "That's a bloody pot plant! Mary-Jane!"

"So what? It's legal."

And nearby, where competition was becoming dire, a strangled cry of anguish arose at the sight of a collection of crushed chrysanthemums in disarray, while beneath the vegetable table a perfectly proportioned potato, a magnificent Yukon Gold specimen, lay mashed before its time.

Things were getting out of hand.

Annabelle Bell-Atkinson became involved in a row with the Clements youngsters when Alun asked if she and her two corgis were entered in the owner-pet look-alike contest. Another fractious moment came when Jillian asked the geeks the same question about them and their newly acquired chimpanzee friend, Cheetah, whom they had named from watching old Johnny Weissmuller Tarzan movies.

The PETA woman told Danny, "You do realize that not only is a chimpanzee not a pet, it has been judged to be almost a person by a New York court. I demand that those two release it."

"Here?" Danny asked. He grinned at the passing speculation of the possibility that such an action could result in one or more local families claiming the creature as a missing member.

Over the way, baked goods were under attack. One of two strawberry-and-rhubarb pies was missing a significant slice, giving it the appearance roughly of a gibbous moon. Danny decided, while pointing no particular finger at the other pie's maker, the often-pugnacious Barbara Baranski, that suspicious circumstances made a prize ruling untenable.

Back with the animals, two lambs brought over by a contestant from Salt Spring panicked when Fatima turned her gaze on them, bounded away at speed, and flattened an iguana belonging to lawyer Ezekial Watson, who howled that he would sue everyone involved in the celebrations, including Harry Dyson for negligence of gate duty.

Silas Cotswold, in *The Tidal Times* the next day, said, "Several attempts to diffuse the various conflicts did little to help."

This set Sheila Martin aflame over a word she saw misused everywhere she looked. The mayor and retired English teacher paraded in front of the newspaper office with a sign that said, "DEFUSE, NOT DIFFUSE! LEARN THE LANGUAGE!"

The vote at the events committee by the presidents of the Spinner's Inlet Owners and Pets Association, the

Spinner's Inlet Gardening Club, and the Cooking and Baking Alliance to go their separate routes in future was unanimous.

Rachel Spinner

Rachel Spinner's phone rang. Its ring tone was the first bars of an old ballad about a legendary huntsman from England's most northwesterly county of Cumberland, which the first Spinners had left to find and name a new home.

> D'ye ken John Peel with his coat so gay,
> D'ye ken John Peel at the break of day,
> D'ye ken John Peel when he's far, far away,
> With his hounds and his horn in the morning . . .

In the kennels behind the house an ageing Irish setter bitch named Fleet raised her head and watched the back door, waiting for her woman to appear with the leash. The phone went to voice mail. In a few minutes the phone rang again, and once more went to voice mail. Fleet whimpered, then settled down, her head resting between her outstretched forelegs, and watched the door. She was the only one remaining of Rachel's long line of setters.

A sudden, sharp breeze off the Strait of Georgia whipped through a stand of willows on the edge of a small pond at the side of the property, found its way under the massive front door, ruffled the drapes, and briefly bothered a framed photograph on the clear-fir-finished wall above the blackened stone fireplace.

A book lay open on the table, a journal of sorts: Rachel's Book of Memories. An old, lovingly polished coal miner's miniature lamp sat near the book. The book was open to the date of the photograph on the wall: Good Friday, 1941.

The familiar photograph was the young Rachel in the blue uniform of a second officer in the British Air Transport Auxiliary, with a pilot's wings. A ferry pilot. Beside Rachel, a slim young man in Royal Air Force blues with flying officer's rings on his sleeves. Jack Thomas.

Rachel had delivered a Spitfire to RAF Biggin Hill. Jack had laughed at her tiny frame as she climbed out of the cockpit. Had stopped laughing when she offered some suggestions. And had fallen in love and declared he would never leave her side.

They had managed a seventy-two-hour pass. He had taken her in his 1937 MG and driven for eight hours, with two stops in small towns in the Lake District, until they arrived at the coal-mining village where the first Spinners—Samson and his young wife, Maud—had left behind a collier's life. The village sat on the moorland between the Irish Sea to the west, and the Lakes to the east.

They went immediately to the local pub, The Greyhound Inn, known to the locals as t' Dog. An old collier set down his pint and said, "Hoosta gaan on, lass? Watt's thy fettle?" It was translated. "He means, how are you going on, how are you doing, how's your health?"

Two strangers. But not for long, as Rachel asked if there were any Spinners there.

"Canadian." The word swirled around the barroom, and into the snug, where three women sat. "A Spinner? By lad! Get up to Number 13."

Which was the home, in the two-street village of ninety houses, of Matt Spinner, his wife, Maggie, and their five children.

While the messenger took off, Rachel was asked by other villagers if she knew their cousins in . . . Winnipeg . . . Dawson Creek . . .

Rachel was given a room in the two-up, two-down Spinner house. "You lot git in together and mek room for yer . . . for our Rachel," with a wide and delighted smile. Jack was put next door.

They handed over their ration books, which were gladly accepted and taken down to the co-op store for a few slices of bacon, some butter, and Spam, from America.

The next day they walked the two hundred yards down to the pit, where a shift of black-faced colliers was just coming off and another was waiting to take the cage down the four hundred feet and onto the coal face.

A line of young and less-young women wearing heavy overalls toiled at long conveyor belts piled with coal, on the pit top. "Screen lasses," it was explained. "They sort the coal from slate and rock." As critical to the war effort as anyone. Maud Skillings had been a screen lass, way back when . . .

They met more Spinners, who never left the area much even now, and who were fascinated to learn what Rachel knew about the original Samson. One of them ("I'm probably a distant fourth cousin or summat") took her to the nearby Church of the Holy Spirit, where an amiable vicar helped them find the record of Samson and Maud's marriage in the summer of 1854. Rachel took a photo of the page.

Matt and Maggie Spinner presented her with a miner's miniature lamp. "Just a laal reminder, lass."

On their return, the RAF regiment corporal at the base gates examined their passes, raised an eyebrow at their being two hours late, then raised the barrier and waved them through with a cheeky, and what he considered to be a knowing, grin.

Jack announced their engagement in the officers mess. They would be married during his next weekend leave. The announcement was enough to kick off a series of parties that lasted past dawn and where they slow danced to Vera Lynn singing "Yours," and Glenn Miller's

"Begin the Beguine." Members of the Women's Land Army were recruited to partner young pilots with no close attachments of their own. They did the hokey-cokey with abandon, as if there were to be no tomorrow.

Which there would not be for so many, when the coming Battle of Britain would provoke Winston Churchill to declare, "Never in the field of human conflict was so much owed by so many to so few."

There was no next leave. Jack for a split-second neglected to check for the infamous "Hun in the sun" while pursuing a Focke-Wulf Fw 190 over the town of Hastings. He was shot down by a Messerschmitt and died in his flaming Spitfire.

Rachel never returned to Cumberland.

The telephone rang again, "D'ye ken John Peel . . ." In the kennel, Fleet raised a hopeful look. The last of the breeze slipped under the door, and the photo on the wall seemed to move once, as if adjusting, then settled back into place.

The phone went to voice mail.

Samson ordered a gravestone for Rachel, for her place in the cemetery at the Church in the Vale. It would have a pilot's wings engraved into it and would read: "Rachel Spinner 1919–2019. Fondly remembered."

Thelma

It seemed as though every ferry carried someone who had arrived for Rachel Spinner's funeral. Most of them had responded to one of the emails sent on Samson's behalf by the Clements twins, who frequently rescued Samson from issues with the computer.

The twins had followed up the emailings by taking up sentry and welcoming-committee duties at the ferry dock, where they latched onto one of the first arrivals. Aunt Jillian—their mother Julie's older sister—was making one of her infrequent return trips to the Inlet. And as the kids fully expected, she arrived from her executive position in

London, England, laden with gifts in colourful bags from the city's best-known shops.

Of course Thelma Spooner arrived, to cry and to bid her old friend goodbye. And of course Thelma drove up to the wedding tree on Ennerdale Road, where once Samson had thwarted the plans of the provincial highways department to bring the ancient maple down. He had organized a "wedding" with himself and Thelma as the principals and had carved their initials and a heart into the thick bark. The carving had joined many more put there since Spinner's Inlet had been named and populated. The highways crew had altered their plans: the new stretch of highway divided and ran around each side of the maple.

Thelma had taken Samson's actions to be a promise that their romance was real and the carving a proposal. Samson seemed to have thought differently. Thelma had moved on from her job at the Spinner's Inlet post office to a promotion and a supervisory position with Canada Post in Calgary.

Samson had watched her arrive off the ferry, had offered a smile, a "How're you doin'?" and a tentative hug, which Thelma returned. They had arrived at the old tree at the same time. He looked sheepish as she traced the carving of their names with a finger. Samson thought Thelma looked much younger than her sixty years. He sucked in his belly and stood straighter. He sighed as he recalled a recent discussion with his young Maritimes relative, Sam Spinner. "Ignoring 'What if?'" he had said then, "and getting on with it is a hell of a sight better than later on saying, 'If only.'"

"Close thing," Thelma offered, nodding to their initials, which were covered by thickening bark.

Samson nodded. "It was." And thought, *Christ!*

Beside them, a slamming of a car door and an overly cheerful voice. "Thelma! I thought it was you." Danny Sakiyama, the apparently ageless letter carrier. "Haven't seen you since Calgary, and wasn't that a night to remember?" He nudged her; Thelma gave him an impatient glance and stepped away.

"I was just saying . . ." Danny turned to Samson.

"I heard you," Samson snapped.

Danny had always been considered a ladies' man. But always short-term. He had never found one he wanted to stay with, nor one who wanted to stay with him, given his reputation.

Samson wondered if Thelma knew that—or if it was any of his concern to wonder.

"He was just saying," Thelma explained, "that we had a couple of drinks last month in Calgary when we were both at a Canada Post Western employees convention. I don't know how late Mr. Sakiyama stayed, but it sounds as though he enjoyed it."

Samson chuckled. Then he took a closer look at Danny. The letter carrier had foregone his standard Canada Post uniform in favour of what, at a stretch, could be called a suit. It was a pinstripe item that might have been in fashion thirty years before. It was ill-fitting, leaving an impression that Danny might have dressed himself during a high wind, and possibly in the dark.

Samson smiled.

Afterward they joined a crowd at the Cedars, people squeezing in among the half-dozen tables, and a few pulling up extra chairs. They shared Rachel Spinner stories and talked of how the funeral had gone.

The cortege had been led by the veterinarian Scott McConville, with Rachel's last setter, Fleet, on a leash in his right hand, and the late Swede's Conrad IV on his left. The dogs had taken to each other, apparently having found a canine camaraderie in a shared sense of loss. Fleet even stopped along the way and showed remarkable patience while Conrad spent a moment at a BC Hydro pole. Constable Ravina Sidhu had taken bugle duty and played a somewhat quavering version of "D'ye Ken John Peel?"—which she had learned from a combined YouTube video and Rachel's cellphone ring tone. This was respectfully received.

Connie Wilson attended, on a week's bereavement leave from the American Musical and Dramatic Academy. She had returned on a business-class ticket. This was a gift from Gilbert Chen who, knowing of Rachel's admiration for the girl's talents, and Rachel's substantial but unheralded contribution to the community's fund to help Connie get to the New York school, had phoned her and said, "Get out to LaGuardia, ASAP." Connie had sung "Amazing Grace" to close the service, and no eye was dry when she finished.

Samson enjoyed seeing the mixture of Spinner's Inlet's population. Ali Hanif was involved in a game of darts with Jack Steele and Finbar O'Toole. Check your wallet, Ali, Samson thought. Ali's wife, Aila, listened to whatever Anwen Brannigan had just said, and laughed aloud. The Hanif kids and a gang of others were lined up at table of soft drinks and cookies. Constable Ravina Sidhu leaned against the back wall, happily overseeing everything.

As Samson watched, Thelma was hugged by Sheila Martin, an old friend, and by Sheila's daughters, Jillian and Julie, who had been toddlers when Thelma ran the post office. She had always had a treat for them behind the counter. And by the Clements twins, who were competing for attention from their Aunt Jillian. Sheila Martin said, "Almost like old times," and wiped the corner of an eye with a tissue. Families.

He noticed Thelma looking at the familiar blue-on-white ferry schedule folded in one hand and then at her wristwatch. The *Gulf Queen* was due in an hour, departing for Swartz Bay. Not that it was ever on time.

Samson also noticed couples. Hyacinth Jakes and Willard Starling from the seniors complex, holding hands and nodding along to the music. Cedars' owner Matthew Blacklock had chosen several Second World War songs from the pub's playlist, for Rachel. Dr. Daisy Chen and Erik Karlsson, the Second Swede, slow dancing in circles off in a tiny corner. Young Sam Spinner and his bride-to-be, Cathy Sloan, soon to be living in the house Rachel had bequeathed to them, linking fingers under their table.

The lawyer Ezekial Watson was being introduced to Thelma by Annabelle Bell-Atkinson, who had assumed a hostess role for the day and who, Samson had to admit, was doing a sterling job of it. She was making sure that no one was left alone, that even outside visitors were being made part of the celebration of Rachel's life, because that's what it had become.

Annabelle had the geeks with her but had suggested they stay in the corner with their laptops and play computer chess. She had decided to watch the pair closely ever since the "Banksy" episode in the village centre. So had Constable Ravina, Annabelle had noticed.

Samson became aware that Danny Sakiyama had insinuated himself into the group alongside Thelma. Danny's voice was never lost in a crowd. Now he was saying to Thelma, "How about them Canada Post layoffs, eh? Wonder who they're coming after?"

Chatter died down. Cameron Girard slipped his notebook out, which got him a nod from Silas Cotswold. Silas had been lauded for a splendid, full-page obituary on Rachel in *The Tidal Times*.

"We're calling the situation 'downsizing,'" Thelma corrected Danny.

Danny frowned, seemed to be puzzled. Then after a few seconds, "You said 'we.' What's that all about?"

Thelma looked up at him. "Danny, you know that I'm part of management now. Perhaps you don't remember?"

Samson snorted. Danny glared at him.

"That's the 'we.' It's a team decision."

Danny nodded slowly. "And how many of the 'team' are being 'downsized'?" he sneered.

"Me, for one," Thelma retorted.

"Christ!" Samson sputtered.

"I'm going to stay with Heather for a while." Heather

was her daughter who, years ago, had moved her riding club to Sidney on Vancouver Island.

People drank up and began drifting away. They stopped when Willie Whittle put down his cellphone and called for attention. "The *Gulf Queen* has been delayed for . . ." His words were lost in the laughter that greeted his announcement. Just like old times.

Delayed. Christ! Samson made for Thelma's group and invited her to step away for a moment. It was much later when he went home. Thelma Spooner accepted an invitation to stay over with Sheila Martin.

The Clements twins got to spend another night with their Aunt Jillian. The next day their presence was required at Samson's place, where he advised them he needed another bunch of emails sent out, invitations to a wedding, which would be held under the ancient maple on Ennerdale Road.

Acknowledgements

Thanks, first and foremost, to my wife June—first reader, thoughtful critic, and story proposer.

To the TouchWood Editions team of dedicated professionals—publisher Taryn Boyd, marketing and publicity coordinator Tori Elliott, editorial co-ordinator Renée Layberry, designer Colin Parks, and proofreader Claire Philipson—I offer my sincere thanks. I must also express gratitude to my always patient (and relentlessly vigilant) editor, Marlyn Horsdal, who as publisher of Horsdal and Schubart brought the first Spinner's Inlet to readers way back when.

I will always remember the Gulf Islanders we knew as part-time residents of Galiano Island. It's been a great pleasure to recall them and their often weird and wonderful outlooks on life.

DON HUNTER grew up in Cumbria, England, attended Workington Grammar School, and served two years with 23 Parachute Field Ambulance before completing teacher training at Chester. He taught for two years before he and his wife, June, immigrated to BC in 1961.

After eight years teaching in BC and gaining a B.Ed. at the University of British Columbia, he switched to journalism and spent almost 30 years with the *Province* newspaper as reporter, editor, and finally senior columnist. He had earlier worked also as a farm labourer, strawberry picker, mail deliverer, taxi driver, longshoreman, construction worker, and screenwriter.

The Hunters built a home on Galiano Island, becoming part-time members of a community whose occupants inspired many of the tales from his original collection of short stories, *Spinner's Inlet*. Don and his wife live in Fort Langley, BC. They have two daughters and three grandchildren.